WATERMELON SNOW

by

Linda Romero Criswell

Branch Office Press
Carbondale, Colorado

ISBN 978-0-359-25227-5

Some of these stories originally appeared *in The Denver Post, Horizons* and *Green Prints. The Journal of Normal Sanger* was purchased at a San Diego yard sale in 1991.

Published by Branch Office Press
Printed and bound in the United States of America

WATERMELON SNOW

SIGN UP SHEET

No one showed up for a morning meeting unless it was breakfast and the boss paid. Thea knew this. And it wasn't just ham and eggs; it was breakfast at the Hotel Jerome, the most elegant dining room in Aspen. Coffee was poured from a silver pot. The orange juice was fresh squeezed and served in crystal stemware. The food menu was no less impressive. Lemon chiffon hotcakes with honey raspberry sauce. Eggs Starwood topped with truffles and golden hollandaise. It was just another cost of business, but business was good at Theodora's Consignments. They were a good team, these girls.

You might think that after ten years together, they'd run out of things to talk about. But in fact, the opposite was true, and that was the reason Thea had called the meeting early on this rainy August morning. The customers were complaining that it might be nice to be *assisted* once in a while, instead of having to wait for Thea's girls to stop talking long enough to take their money. Only yesterday, Barb had been the guilty party, giving Katie the Wardrobe Talk when she should have been ringing up a sale. "You ought to ditch those long skirts," she suggested. "If I had your legs, I wouldn't hide them like that." To illustrate her point, Barb held out the hem of her swingy black silk mini-skirt and wiggled her curvy hips.

"I like long skirts. I can wear tights under them," Katie argued. "Tights last longer than panty hose. They're a better deal. Besides, if you look sexy, you attract jerks."

"And your shoes. They are so dated. Isn't this their third year?"

"Do you think I could get a little service around here?" a well-dressed tourist asked, clicking the corner of her credit card on the glass counter.

"Don't count on it," one of the regular customers answered her. "This isn't the kind of place where they wait on you. This is Theodora's. You want service, go to Chanel. But it'll cost you ten times as much."

Nevertheless, Thea, the owner, wanted her girls to put the customer first. Slim and graceful, her short blond hair cut by the same stylist who used to do Cher, her makeup expertly applied, Thea wore a chocolate off-the-shoulder cashmere sweater and matching silk trousers set off by a heavy gold chain necklace and enormous earrings. Thea's costume would have been appropriate for a Manhattan cocktail party, but this was her work uniform, purchased from the racks of her own fashionable, if second hand, boutique. "Even if you're talking about something really important," she continued, "stop chatting and help the buyer first. Finish your story later," she said. "Katie's good at that."

"Yeah, but she dresses like a bag lady," Barb said in a loud stage whisper. Katie responded by sticking out her tongue. Thea rolled her eyes. Sometimes they were more like a class of adolescents, not a team of forty-ish women who helped her run the best consignment store in the West.

"And let's be very, very careful this season about checking for spots and missing buttons. We want to keep our reputation for having perfect merchandise. Okay?" Thea said.

Everyone nodded, grateful not to have been singled out. Thea glanced at the clock. "That's all I have to say. Does anyone have anything to add?" she asked.

Katie held up an index finger. "I have a teeny suggestion," she said.

"Show off," Barb hissed, smiling.

"Quiet," said Katie. She looked around the room at the other women. "Most of us have been here at Theodora's a long time. We're not getting any younger. Anita here is forty-three, Charlotte is, well, we all know Charlotte is *real* old." Charlotte glared. "And this is a high pressure job. Dealing with customers, pricing, watching for shoplifters, handling the money." It was not unusual, they all knew, for a single shopper at Theodora's to spend a thousand dollars in an afternoon.

The women became quiet. At the same moment, they all realized that Katie was about to make a pitch to Theodora for a raise for all of them. No one had ever dared to do that before. They sat perfectly, surprisingly still.

You could hear the clock ticking.

But instead, Katie held up a piece of notebook paper. "So I thought we should have this schedule," she said. She held the paper high, for everyone to see. *Menopause Sign Up Sheet*, it read. "Some of you are awfully close," Katie said, smiling innocently. "I won't mention any names, but you know who you are. Here's how it works: everyone gets a year, no more, no less. In that year, no one else gets to be menopausal; just the person who signed up. When your year's over, that's that. Lighten up. No more excuses."

"Since Charlotte is the oldest and crankiest, she probably needs next year, so I've put her name down already. See if you can control yourself until January, Char," she said. "We don't start till then." Everyone laughed, even Char.

"I myself think I have six more years to go, so I'm signing up for that year right now. I'll pass this around and you can fill in your name next to the year you want. No doubling up, now. There's enough for everybody."

"Is she serious?" the new girl whispered to Barb.

"Oh, yes," Barb said. "I'll take the year after Katie's," she announced, raising a carefully-manicured hand, her silver bracelets jingling.

"I want two years, okay?" asked Mona.

"No," said Katie. "Rules are rules."

"You're already a bitch," said Charlotte. You're already *had* your two years."

Thea breathed a sigh of relief. "I love you all," she said, as she did after every meeting. "Now let's get out of here and open up. We start taking skiwear today. It'll be a zoo."

NORMAN SANGER, 1915 A.D.

"What's all that stuff in that box?" Thea asked later that morning. "Looks like garage sale leftovers."

"Somebody from Switchback wants to put it on consignment," Katie said. "She works across the street at the dentist's."

"Switchback. That's an hour's drive every day."

"As a matter of fact," Katie said, "I'm going to be making it myself soon. I signed a lease on a little house up there, one of those old miner's cabins. I'm moving on the first of September, in two weeks. In time to plant tulips. I think. Aren't they the ones you plant in the fall and they come up in the spring?"

"You're moving? That's the end of the earth, Switchback. They don't even get cable. Just that weird radio station."

"It's too expensive for me to live in Aspen," Katie said. "Now that Eric's in college, I can move a little farther away. Somewhere cheaper."

"Do you think you'll ever get back with You-Know-Who?" asked Thea.

"Not since he told me I have a better chance of being stuck by lightning than getting married since I'm over forty."

"Well, that's what they say around here."

"No comment," Katie answered.

"You're still going to work here, aren't you?" Thea asked. "I need you." Thea looked out at the shop, already filling with customers at this early hour. Although the business was housed in an 1880s Victorian cottage, tiny by Aspen standards and one of the last surviving old houses in town, the elegance of the merchandise more than made up for the rustic interior.

"Oh, sure. I'll just have a longer commute," Katie said. "Lots of people do it, and I'm going to have to pay rent now, like all the worker bees."

"Not like living for free with You-Know-Who," Thea said.

"Leon. His name was Leon. *Is* Leon. And living with him was not exactly free," said Katie. She reached into the box of housewares. "There's some nice stuff in here. China teacups. Picture frames. Must've belonged to one of those old miners from Switchback." She lifted out a crumbling leather-covered notebook and opened the cover carefully. "Listen to this," she said.

Private Property
To those with honor keep out.
Those without honor look out!
1915 A.D. --Norman Sanger

"The pages are all brittle," Thea said. "Throw it away. We don't take junk."

"Mind if I keep it?" Katie asked.

"Be my guest."

Katie turned the fragile handwritten pages with care. "It looks like a collection of essays," she said. "Here's one called *"How to Live a Longer and Happier Life"*. Or how about this one? *"The Moral Coward."*

"Sounds like a preacher," Thea said.

"Maybe. Actually, though, it looks exactly like the stuff I used to write in high school. I was such an idealist," said Katie.

"You don't say," Thea said dryly, remembering how Katie pestered every winter season her to stop selling fur coats in the shop, even though they were one of her best money makers.

Katie ran her hand over the cracked cover of the notebook. "I'll bring this up to Switchback and read it on a cold winter night in front of the wood stove," Katie said. "To feed my hungry spirit."

"It sounds like something What's-His-Name would do," answered her boss.

"Leon didn't read," Katie said. "Unless it was *TV Guide.*"

"Not Leon. The other guy. The old one. The writer guy. Norman Sanger."

FRUITS OF LABOR

I have written herein about things in general--not for anyone's entertainment but my own. These little jaunts of my pen are crude affairs. But just beyond lies another field, accessible to one if he dares to venture there.

Katie closed the yellowed journal and squinted into the distance from a chair she'd placed outside her cabin door. Near treeline up on Echo Mountain to the south, golden aspens glowed as brightly as fire. Her move to Switchback only two weeks ago had been easy and fast. How much stuff can you squeeze into a one-bedroom shack, anyway? Everything fit easily into Theodora's borrowed pickup truck, with room left over.

Through the weather-beaten fence, Katie peeked at her neighbor, skinny old Ida Contino, whom she met the day she moved in. As usual, Ida propelled herself through her yard with a slight forward lean. It was a hot day for Switchback, which meant it was like cool day anywhere else. Thin air holds little heat, but weather is not something that surprises Ida anymore. She visits her tidy vegetable garden, four straight rows of strawberries. "Dig one up and plant one new every year," she says. She checks in with her spuds, lettuce beds, and beets. She pulls up a tiny clump of crabgrass and snaps off a brown leaf, putting it in the pocket of her faded yellow apron.

Ida, at age ninety-one, is not the oldest resident of Switchback, Colorado. She is not even the oldest person on 8th Street, because Oscar Rohde lives only one block to the north of her, and he turned a healthy one hundred last January. Ida is a Catholic and Oscar is a Mormon, and this leads some citizens of Switchback to wonder if perhaps there is a connection between living by the Good Book and living long. Ella Thacker, after all, is a suspected atheist--she swears and smokes and is never seen in church except for the Seniors Free Wednesday Lunch at St. Teresa's--and she had to move into Resurrection Nursing Home at the relatively young age of seventy-six. The family sold her house to pay the bills. Ida and Oscar still live in their own houses. It's not hard to draw conclusions.

Ida walked over to the chokecherry bush in the corner of her yard. A heavy frost in late spring killed off the delicate flowers. No flowers, no fruit. "No problem," said Ida to herself. She still has plenty of jelly left over from the bumper crop of 1995 in her root cellar.

Ida can no longer hear well, but in the old days when Ernie was alive, they would listen for the day of the bees, that one day in May when the chokecherry blossoms were the sweetest and the bees came, one to every flower. Their sound was so loud you could even hear it from inside the house. Ida and Ernie drew up stools directly beneath the sweet-smelling branches and sat in silence, smiling at each other, while the bush hummed so loudly it went right to their hearts, that song.

Ida's lawn is the most perfect in Switchback, a seamless carpet of green. On her daily inspections, she picks up each fallen leaf, pulls every dandelion foolish enough to raise its head to take a look around. She has a rechargeable electric lawn mower that growls like a mountain lion as it leads her up and down the rows, snipping every blade of grass to the exact height of one-and-one-half inches.

Ida gets her picture in *The Tailings,* Switchback's weekly newspaper, once a year, wisps of snow-white hair peeking out from under her wide-brimmed straw hat, a trowel in her hand. A rookie photographer will usually spot her on his way to the Town Hall to cover a meeting of the Trustees. He will think he's the first to discover her, this wrinkled garden troll, but every *Tailings* photographer since the paper's inception in 1961 has a photograph of Ida in his portfolio. Few people have ever seen a picture of Ida in her youth, but in old age she is very photogenic in a black-and-white sort of way. She stands perfectly still, she never smiles, and she makes page one every spring. This year's picture was captioned, "Garden Angel," and Ida thinks she looks quite good in it, although the caption embarrasses her, suggesting as it does that she's as cute as a cherub, which is not the case. "When you're not purty when you're young, you don't get ugly so quick," she says with a certain pride.

Ida watched Katie move in next door two weeks ago, wheeling her few possessions down the walk with a beat-up furniture dolly, her shoulder-length brown hair falling into her eyes. She peeked through the slats in the high wooden fence into the jungle of sunflowers and sagebrush that made up Katie's yard. Katie, she has observed, lets anything grow if it looks like it might bloom. Even thistles.

It is clear to Ida that Katie is no gardener. She'll never make it in this town unless she gets down on her knees and yanks out all that bindweed. Last week, Ida watched Katie pull a few clumps of crabgrass, but then, right in the middle of the job, Katie just toppled over and rolled onto her back, staring motionless at the sky. A hard-working person like Ida, when she sees a woman lying so still when there is work yet to be done, she thinks the woman is dead. As she stood there wondering whether to call 911 or go over and feel for a pulse, Ida saw Katie reach out and pet the cat, who was walking by with a moth in its mouth. Ida sniffed and went back to her radishes.

Ida peeked out from behind her kitchen curtains when Katie had her girlfriends over one Saturday, a noisy bunch, sounded like a bunch of chickens, and all gussied up with fancy hats and makeup. They carried the kitchen table outside, lit candles when it grew dark and drank a lot of wine. No one seemed to mind that the pokeweed was going to seed, or that the grass was so long it could be parted like a hairdo. Ida doesn't exactly mind, but she watches the fence line vigilantly, on the lookout for migrating bindweed. When she thinks no one is looking, she slips a scrawny hand under the fence and yanks the culprits from Katie's lawn, before they invade her own perfect turf.

On Sunday morning, Ida *tsked* at the messy table in Katie's yard, visible through a low knothole in the wooden fence between the two women's homes. She watched as a magpie flew overhead with a crusty piece of cheese clamped in its bill. The magpie flew to Ida's apple tree, knocking off a piece of ripe fruit as it landed. "That does it," Ida said out loud. She headed resolutely over to Katie's.

"You said you were going to come and pick those apples yesterday," Ida said, hands on her skinny hips.

"Oh my gosh," Katie said. "I forgot. I'll be right over." She looked up at the sky. "Looks like a storm is coming in."

"Good. We need it," said Ida. "The ditch is getting low. Now let's get moving."

Back under the apple tree, Ida handed Katie a long pole with a stuff wire hook at one end. "Use this shaker," she directed, and Katie looped the bent end over a branch and shook it hard, hoping no apples would fall on Ida's head and knock her out. Katie was very careful around Ida. She didn't want to be responsible for harming her through some inadvertent act of carelessness. That's the kind of thing they talk about for years to come in a place like this. People might politely avoid the subject at the funeral, but there would still be whispering later on, which would stop when you came into the room. Katie might even have to move away, start a new life elsewhere...but where? Didn't

Thea call this place the end of the earth? Where can you go after that?

"Why don't you step back a little, Ida?" Katie said. Ida complied.

"This is sure a beautiful tree," remarked Katie.

"It's from when we were first married," Ida replied. "Ernie's brother came down from Saskatchewan and brought us a bushel of apples from his farm. We threw the cores in the compost and some of them sprouted. This one here is the only one that took when I transplanted it." She placed her hand protectively on a low branch.

A sizzle of lightning made them both jump, and in an instant the sky broke into a downpour. The two women moved in closer to the trunk of the ancient tree.

The wind picked up suddenly, shaking loose a shower of twigs and leaves. Rain fell in sheets around them, but the thick canopy of branches overhead kept Ida and Katie dry.

They stood for a long time, watching. Across the street, plastic lawn chairs blew into lilac bushes, their blooms long gone. Trash can lids slid noisily across driveways. The rain came hard and cold now, making a circular wall around them, like a sheer curtain, closing in the place where they stood. The branches formed an almost watertight roof over their heads.

Ida smiled up at Katie, as if the two of them shared a secret. "It's nice under here," she said.

"I know," smiled Katie. Nothing else needed to be said.

In a few minutes the storm was over, passing through the small town in a matter of seconds and thundering down the valley. "In another month, it'll be snow, not rain," Ida said. "I'll bet you the top of Echo Mountain will be white tomorrow morning."

Ida let Katie give her the most tentative of hugs, one gentle enough not to do any damage. Ida stiffened a little at first, but then relaxed, stretching her arms around the tall woman in a way that was almost shy. "Thank you," Katie said. She balanced the basket of apples on her hip and slowly walked to her own back door. She set the basket on the back porch and sat down beside it on the step. The sun broke through the clouds. The kitten rubbed against her ankles, and then took off after a grasshopper. Bees hummed in the purple comfrey flowers.

Katie started to think about tomorrow, another work day. What to wear, what to take for lunch, what to do about dinner when she arrived home on the bus after dark. Twelve hours every day she was away from home, to get her nine hours in at the Aspen consignment shop.

Katie thought about a conversation she'd had on the bus when she first moved to Switchback. "How are you dealing with the long commute?" a woman had asked her.

"I guess I should start looking for work here in Switchback." Katie answered. "But I like my job."

"Don't worry," the woman said kindly. "I'm sure the second-hand store over on Main will have an opening soon. They have a big turnover. With your experience, they'd love you."

But I can do other things, too, thought Katie. I can type. I can make clothing, or keep books, or write for a newspaper. But she kept quiet, thinking: Will my obituary say 'well-liked retail salesperson?' Is that what people will remember?

Katie looked down at her bushel of apples. She left them on the step and went inside the house. Light shone onto the table where a notebook lay, open to a blank page. Pulling her messy hair into a bun and fastening it with a rubber band, Katie began to write:

Today I stood with Ida under a Saskatchewan apple tree in a thunderstorm

THE POSSESSIVE FORM

Make your life like a sweet dream.
                              --Norman Sanger

Two days later, Katie sat in her car and chewed on the end of her pen as she watched a rusty pickup truck rattle toward Switchback on Evelyn Store Road. The pavement snaked through cottonwood groves and across irrigation ditches before veering sharply to the left, and then, just a few yards further on, it reached the top of the rise that led down to Main Street at the old railroad crossing. On maps, Evelyn Store Road is identified as County Road 154, but no one from Switchback would call it that. If you did, people would get lost, not know which road you were talking about. Just call it Evelyn Store. Not Evelyn's Store with an S. Just Evelyn. Period. Katie hadn't been in town long enough to know where the name came from. She wrote in her notebook: *Evelyn Store. Why?*

Katie wasn't around when Mrs. Poole, the English teacher, started a campaign to add an apostrophe-and-s to the name of the store and the road. "It is a bad example for our children to perpetuate this grave grammatical offense," she wrote in a letter to *The Tailings*. She didn't think it was funny at all when her students responded by dropping the possessive in their everyday speech as well, just to get her goat.

"I would like to pick up Sam homework," said one of them slyly. "He's reading that Plato Republic."

"Plato's," Mrs. Poole corrected. "Oh, hell. I give up."

Katie took a sip of soda out of the can she'd brought along and sat back against the driver's seat to enjoy the view. For transportation, she took the bus or rode her bike, but when she wanted a nice, warm, private place away from the four walls of her cabin, Katie preferred her gold-colored 1994 Toyota.

Of all the things Katie did in her car, eating was her favorite. She often made herself a sandwich and drove out to a place with a good view to eat it. Katie's old boyfriend, Leon, ate lunch in front of the television, and in all fairness Katie had to admit that eating in the car might be just as degenerate, although the view was better up here on County Road 154. Katie liked the feeling of efficiency that came from doing more than one thing at a time. Multi-tasking, they called it.

Katie figured that she was a good multi-tasker, because she could eat an apple while she walked to the hardware store and listened to a radio interview over her headphones. Three things at once. What a time saver, she told herself proudly, although she's not exactly sure what she's saving time *for*.

Sometimes Katie meditates in her car; it's quiet and warm. There are no phones to ring, no clocks ticking. Once you maneuver your legs around the steering wheel, you can sit in a lotus position for half an hour if you like. The most that might happen is someone raps on your window and asks, "Are you ok?" and you say yes, you are just meditating, and then they leave you alone. You can get away with doing what you like in Switchback, once they get to know you. They trust you more if you have a quirk or two. It makes you normal, more approachable.

Occasionally Katie snaps photographs of the sights that she sees through her windshield, the grainy texture of her pictures caused by the ever-present dust clinging to the glass. She keeps her camera in the car all the time now, under a Mexican blanket. You never know when the light is going to hit the cottonwoods just right along Evelyn Store Road. You want to be ready. Katie is ready for something, she thinks, but it's not another so-called relationship. She feels stupid enough already.

In what Katie calls her former life, she lived with a man in his house in Aspen. It was not *her* house, something Leon reminded her of the day she put her grandmother's porcelain owl on the bookshelf. "Everything has to be magical," he told her, removing the owl and placing it in a drawer. They shopped together for meaningful accessories and Leon told people, "It cost me a fortune to ship this back from Paris," as if the price of the thing would make it more beautiful. Leon composed the rooms of his house as if he were setting the stage for a play. A sterling box here, a sculpture there. And indeed, it *was* beautiful; one could hardly wait for the actors to arrive. Not one to grasp things quickly, Katie took years to realize that she, too, was simply part of the decor.

"I thought if I played the role well, I'd get to keep it without re-auditioning all the time," she said to him.

"What you see is what you get," Leon said, an expression he found useful in ending most relationships.

"Well, I haven't gotten a thing out of this," said Katie. "I just wish it hadn't taken me six years to realize it."

"What do you mean? You get to be with *me!*" said Leon, incredulous. "With no strings! What could be better? Besides, remember the odds. You have a better chance of being struck by lightning than…"

But she was out the driveway, leaving a dark patch of rubber on his precious cobblestones, for which he will gladly tell you what he paid. It was a fortune, because he brought the mason over from Tuscany. "Old World crafts-men are the only ones who know how to do it right," he explains to anyone who will listen.

Here on Evelyn Store Road, Katie observed, they did it right, too, without the fanfare. They let the fence posts weather to a shiny pewter-colored patina. They let the potato shed that Ida and her brothers built years ago crumble away in its own time. They placed single geranium plants in kitchen windows, the blood-red blossoms contrasting with old lace curtains the color of clouds.

Katie watched as one lonely turkey buzzard circled the rodeo grounds, its wings inscribing a smooth V against the darkening sky. She wrote:

The best time in Switchback is in middle October, when the sun is low. Mornings are as still as sleep. The grass crackles under your feet; your nose and hands freeze. Evenings are sweeter, with the honk of geese, with the gentle sound of cars pulling out of gravel driveways. Even before the elms and the aspens change, the bushes turn red and gold. The scrub oak is the color of a campfire, the whole spectrum of flame and shadow. In the meadows along Evelyn Store Road, the bales of hay get crisp around the edges and their shadows are sharp, black against emerald fields.

Winter brings the browns, but that's still weeks away. For now, in autumn's last, wild burst of color, Switchback blends its hues with the flair of a master impressionist and then tones them down with a sprinkle of snow. The red willows against the bluest of rivers create a lavender you may only see again in heaven, or at least not until you pass this way again.

In some places it is spring that makes a man reach for his fly rod when he gets home from work and cast his hook into a bend of the river. But here, it's fall. Stand on Evelyn Store Bridge and watch a solitary fisherman tasting the final moments of day, his line looking as delicate as a golden strand from the web of a spider. Soon the sun will drop behind Red Mountain and he will be chilled to the bone. Daylight is precious this time of year.

It is fall when the housewife turns off the stew, pulls on her boots and walks along Eagle Gulch one last time before winter sets in. She knows where the enormous birds have their nest. If she stands just beneath it in the shadows, she might see them coming to roost for the night; she might hear the whoosh of their gigantic wings as they land, reaching for the branch with claws the size of a cattle roper's hands. And, because the low angle of October sun reminds her how fast the daylight is shrinking, she takes this moment to fill her eyes with all of it, enough to last all the frozen months ahead.

If you come to Switchback in the fall, they say, you will find it difficult ever to leave. Move here in October and you are a goner. You might as well plant a slow-growing bristlecone pine in your front yard, because you will never leave this place; it is as close to home as you will ever come, probably. Some feel blessed by its hold on them; others feel cursed. Either way, they always seem to come back. There is no easy way out, not if you belong here.

Experiencing fall at timberline is like having a new pair of glasses. All of a sudden, you can see every brown blade of grass, every ragged wash of violet in the sky. For a day or two, or maybe for the whole season if you are good at this, you go around with a new, detailed, wondering point of view, and the colors and shapes all but wash the inside of your head with radiance. Sometimes you can live off this all winter, if you are careful not to fuss with it. Sometimes, you can make it last.

MY TOWN, COLORADO

Our homes ought to be our heaven on earth.
--Norman Sanger

Katie heard about it from Sage's own mother, Jane Wozniak, in the alley on trash day. "Why can't she just string toilet paper in the principal's tree on Halloween like everyone else?" Jane complained, slamming down the lid on the garbage can. "No, when *my* daughter plays a practical joke, the district attorney gets called in. The police knock on my door. They're talking lawsuit, that real estate company is. Sometimes I think Switchback is just too...well, too *small* for her, you know?"

"Adolescence is God's way of helping us to separate from our children without remorse," said Katie, thinking of her son, Eric, now away at college. "If they stayed cute and adorable, we'd never let them leave home."

It had all started innocently enough, Jane explained. Sage planned to make a brochure for art class. She told Mrs. Swanson the title would be *My Town, Colorado*. Sage explained that she was going to take pictures of her favorite spots in Switchback and make "kind of a pamphlet. Like, for advertising, you know?" she said to her teacher. Mrs. Swanson approved of the project. Sage had been a problem of late. She came in after lunch smelling of cigarette smoke. She had a nail in her eyebrow, not a gold ring like some of the girls, but a regular, half-inch long stainless steel *nail*. It was hard not to stare at it. "My God," said her grandmother. "What kind of boy will ask you out on a date with *that*?" The kind of boy was Hector Montoya, who had a stud in his tongue and bleached the tips of his hair blond, but Sage didn't see the point of bringing him around to meet the folks. Hector got enough grief at home already, Sage figured. Why expose him to more? Especially her embarrassingly friendly mother who would try to make cheerful small talk with him, like some robotic mom in a 1960s rerun. Hector was too good a friend for Sage to do that to him.

Sage got up early the last Saturday of October. It was one of those somber days when snow clouds hang in the air like dirty, wet sponges. She pulled on the irrigation boots she bought for the homecoming dance and slogged out to the power station on the highway. The tall transformer towers reminded her of the creatures in *War of the Worlds*, a movie she once watched on late-night TV. They loomed against the dark sky like the spires of ancient church steeples. Sage held her camera inside the chain link fence and snapped several pictures.

She went across the highway to Switchback's original shopping mall, now a strip of mostly-vacant stores with paint peeling from the door frames. She took a picture of Wild Bill's Tattoo Parlor and another one of the Guns 'n' Jewels Pawnshop. She got a good shot of Marta's Convenient Store, with its colorful pyramid of Blessed Virgin of Guadalupe candles in the window. She would come back later, she decided, and buy one for Hector's grandmother.

Sage snapped a shot of the twelve identical modular houses which stood side by side, not unlike the Army barracks her brother described from boot camp. *Who lets those real estate developers get away with this crap, anyway?* she wondered.

She went north on Eighth Street to where it crossed the train tracks, and there she turned and walked along the rails, passing the back yards of triplexes in the Ruby Red subdivision. Someone had thrown a Christmas tree down the embankment last year, and tinsel still hung from brown, dead branches. She photographed it. A dilapidated dog-house. A dirty yellow sleeping bag that looked like a place a cat would go to have kittens. Cinders. Trash.

Sage took a picture of the line of trailers on the east end of Wilson Avenue, at the base of the hill. Mrs. Bosco had stuck new fake flowers from the Ben Franklin store in her window box out front. The Ramirez kid had left his broken plastic wagon by the mailboxes again. A mangy dog stood staring. Click. Click. Click. The camera snapped.

Sage took her time setting up a picture of the sewage treatment plant behind the propane company office. She climbed over the fence to shoot what first appeared to be a placid pond surrounded by wispy goldenrods. Or so she hoped. In a way, the huge, round propane tanks in the background looked a little like cows in a pasture.

The following week, Sage stayed up every night using the computer at her father's architectural office to design her color brochure. She agonized over the wording of the title. It had to have just the right tone. Nothing suspicious. Nothing weird. She eliminated her first choices: *Switchback...Small Town, Big Future*, and *Switchback...Where The New West Meets Old World Charm*. Ugh. She finally settled on *Switchback...a Place to Call Home*. She liked the ring of it. It had been *her* home for her whole life.

Mrs. Wilburn, the math teacher, thought Sage was messy because the homework papers she turned in were covered with peanut butter stains and cigarette burns. She gave Sage a D, which she fully deserved, the semester she failed to complete a single assignment but managed to pass the final. Sage didn't much see the point in math. But she took herself very, very seriously when she was working on her own creations, like this one. She spent every night that week in her father's office, completely focused on her task. Hector brought her a soda and some popcorn but she brushed him away with a wave of her hand, lost in the creative process.

The photographs turned out so well. The colors were rich and pure, with the deep purple Switchback sky above, the terra cotta hills below. The bright yellow of the castaway sleeping bag contrasted artistically with the rough gray texture of the cinders by the tracks. The shiny tinsel on the discarded Christmas tree glittered like gossamer. Under its photo, Sage captioned, "Holidays in Switchback." She felt her idea take shape.

It was just luck that the picture of the electrical substation looked, at a glance, like a stately cathedral against a sinister sky. "Nuclear Power Plant," Sage typed below it. And the waste treatment facility--was that a mountain pond? It looked so pastoral. Was that a herd of white Charolais cattle grazing in the foreground? "Sewage Treatment is now our #1 Priority," typed Sage as a caption. You had to look closely to see the sludge floating on the surface of the water and to notice that those fat four-legged creatures were actually a herd of plump propane tanks.

The picture of the deteriorating modular buildings was splendid. If you didn't look too hard, you might think they were modern apartments. Sage typed beneath the picture "Plenty of Housing for All" and smiled at the torn screen flapping in a broken window.

It was the colorful blooms in Mrs. Bosco's flower box that Sage finally chose for the front of the brochure. At first glance, it looked like an English cottage garden. You didn't immediately notice that the blossoms were plastic. You really had to look. And when you did, you might pick out the stenciled letters...*DYNAMITE*...on the wooden window box screwed onto the side of her trailer. Cliff Bosco had worked at the Ruby Mine for sixteen years as a blaster and often brought home mementos from his job.

The artwork completed, Sage began the task of composing the text. She titled one section *Switchback Myths Debunked*, creating a bulleted list:

- No, the drinking water here doesn't make you fat. That is just a rumor.
- The funny smell usually goes away by November.
- Except for the gang problem, Switchback is a great place to raise a family.

Then, The following evening she worked on the question-and-answer section:

- *Do the horse flies carry disease?*
Nothing serious, as long as you rub some fresh urine on the bites.
- *How cold does it get up there, anyway?*
We don't know exactly. Standard thermometers only reach fifty below.
- *When are they going to clean up the highway?*
After they take care that hazardous waste spill over at the reservoir.

Almost as an afterthought, Sage added a phone number to the back page. You have to let your readers know whom to call for more information, she reasoned. Sage typed in the number of Dean Blevins, Mega Realty's biggest broker, the one who once called Switchback an "uncut jewel" in an interview in the *Denver Post.*

Sage leaned back in the squeaky office chair and proofread her handiwork one last time. She photocopied it, five hundred copies, using her dad's account at the print shop, and folded them neatly into thirds. Then she called

Hector to see if he wanted to hang out on Saturday. Hector's brother, she knew, would lend him the car.

Hector and Sage stopped at every brochure rack between Aspen and Vail. Hector engaged the gas station attendants and hotel clerks in conversation while Sage slid her glossy Switchback brochure into their racks. They stood alongside fliers advertising Quarter-Acre Lots in Paradise, Ski-In Ski-Out Condos, and Coyote Hot Tubs. Sage was proud to see her work among them.

Sage failed to get an A in the project, for all she cared. Mrs. Swanson, whose husband was the mayor, wrote in the margin: *My husband and I do not see the humor in this.*

"Duh," said Sage.

Sage applied to a small independent college in Oregon and sent the brochure to them as an example of her schoolwork. "Ecology?" said her grandmother. "In my day, we didn't have ecology. We had home economics. What good is ecology?" Sage got a scholarship and packed her bags for the Northwest.

No one knows where it is now, Sage's brochure. The dean of admissions sent it to a friend of his, an environmental lawyer in Alaska. It resurfaces occasionally, blurred from copying and recopying, around the West. Mostly it gets tossed into the trash. Dean Blevins is still in business, but a surprising number of his clients refuse to look at the properties he has listed in Switchback, Colorado. And they never, ever drink the water.

HENRY

We arise in the morning with the whole day before us; it is ours to make it as we will.

--Norman Sanger

Easy enough for Norman Sanger to say on a hot summer day, thought Katie, checking the date of his entry-- June 12, 1913. Outside her own window, the blowing January snow obliterated everything except the stark plank fence between her yard and Ida's. She poured a cup of coffee and emptied her last drop of milk into the cup. It was a day for making soup, but there was no food in the house. Still, even in this storm, the grocery store was only a ten-minute walk down a snowpacked sidewalk. She threw on her parka and pulled the hood up over her head.

In the entry to Switchback Soopers, Henry Lind rocked from one foot to the other, waiting for people to admire his new puppy. A black lab named Smoky, the dog rolled over onto his back every time a new person stopped to pet him. He stuck his oversized paws into the air and wriggled. His tail wagged so hard it hit the floor like the sound of gloved hands slapping together to keep warm.

Smoky was one of those smiling dogs. A mean dog could never have that look. A mean dog might grimace at you and at first you think it's a smile, but then he'll lift that little piece of lip and show you his long, sharp tooth, and you know it wasn't a smile at all, but a snarl, and you'd better not get any closer. Not Smoky, though. When Smoky smiles, you can tell he means it. There isn't a dishonest bone in his body. In that way he is like his master.

"He's so cute," said Hillary, who left her post at the checkout stand to scratch Smoky's velvety ears. She bent down and kissed the top of his head. "He still has that new puppy smell," she said to Henry. Some new things are just like that. There's new car smell and new baby smell. Hillary, being sixteen, thinks new puppy smell is the best one of all. She's an only child and hasn't smelled a new baby yet.

Belinda Fisk walked in covered with snow, carrying a poster to tack up on the bulletin board. "Henry! You got a new dog!" she said.

"His name's Smoky," Henry said. He thought he should know the lady's name but he didn't. She often stops to talk to him. He does know her husband, Patrick, because Henry mows their lawn on Saturdays in the summer, and Patrick usually brings out a pitcher of lemonade and drinks it on the front porch with him. Saturday, he knows, is the day that Patrick's wife has her own show on KSWT, the local radio station. "Afternoon of a Housewife," she calls it, and she plays Judy Collins songs, and Alison Krauss. Ladies' stuff. His mom listens to it. Patrick usually has the radio tuned to his wife's show, unless there is a ball game going on in Denver.

Henry has never had a wife or a girlfriend or even a date. It has nothing to do with his appearance, which is ordinary but not unattractive. Last birthday, he turned forty-five. "He has the mind of a six year old," some people say, but what they mean is a sixth *grader*. That seems to be closer to the truth. No one knows, no one can remember at least, why Henry is the way he is. Nor can most people remember when he and his mother came to town, it was that long ago.

Henry and his mom live in a blue two-bedroom trailer with a vegetable garden out front. She is a quiet woman, with short gray hair and patient blue eyes. Mrs. Lind does bookkeeping at home, at a desk in their living room. Years ago someone gave her a computer and she read the manual and took a course at night school, and now she keeps books for the frame shop, the bakery, and Marta's Convenient Store. Henry mows lawns in the summer and shovels snow in the winter. He doesn't do this as a junior high school boy might, picking up an odd job here and there when he needs money for a movie. This is Henry's career. "You'd better think twice before hiring some kid to take Henry's job away from him," the locals advise newcomers to town. It's OK to mow your own lawn in Switchback, or get your boys to shovel the walk, but you certainly wouldn't want to hire anyone but Henry to do the job for pay. It might be seen as mean-spirited.

"Cute puppy," said Belinda, scratching Smoky's ears. Where's Panda?" Belinda knows the dogs and cats in town by name because she is chairman of the KSWT membership drive, during which people are encouraged to purchase additional memberships for their pets. Panda had been a member for years.

"I guess you might be noticing that something is missing," Henry said to Belinda. He spoke stiffly, as if he had practiced his lines at home that morning, which he had.

"Yes. Panda is missing," Belinda said. "Did you leave her at home today?"

"Panda had to be put away," recited Henry, repeating what his mother had told him. "She had a tumor."

"Oh, Henry, I'm so sorry. We will all miss her. She was such a nice dog."

Henry nodded. "We got Smoky at the pound," he said. "I like him pretty much. Mom says I have to train him to heel." With his lawn mower to push all over town once summer comes, Henry needs a dog that will follow him without a leash.

Henry and his mother have had to move three times in the last two years. It wasn't a matter of them not paying the rent or anything. They were good tenants. It was just that Switchback grew, and Mrs. Lind and Henry kept getting caught in the crossfire. The last three places they lived were sold to developers, the mobile homes torn down to make room for houses. Trailers, the developers argued, were eyesores that should be replaced by lovely "high-end" homes. It would improve the quality of the neighborhood, increase property values. Bring a more desirable class of people to town--people who like things nice, people more like themselves.

The third time Henry and his mom were forced to move, someone brought their problem to the attention of the Town Council, which voted unanimously to rent them a permanent trailer space on town-owned land. The council could have found someone who would pay more for it, housing being what it is, but what would have been the point? Their chances of reelection would have been pretty slim if they'd refused to help someone as popular as Henry. Now Henry and his mom pay one dollar a year for the privilege of occupying this spot by the ball field, and Henry keeps the snow shoveled off the bleachers all through the fall season. People tell him he does a good job.

Belinda said she'd keep an eye on Smoky so Henry could go inside and buy his lunch. He walked over to take a look at the soup and salad bar. Beets, raisins, cantaloupe, lots of stuff his mom never put in salads, but it all looked good. Most days of the week, Henry bought his lunch here with some of the money he had made. Soup seemed like the best thing to eat this cold day, even better than a sandwich from the deli case. Besides, Henry was still full from the muffin a customer had given him earlier, insisting that he eat it at her kitchen table after he shoveled her sidewalk.

No one knew the man who shoved Henry aside to grab a paper bowl and slop a ladle of chili into it. "The sonofabitch just fired me," he declared to Henry, the only person within hearing distance.

"Huh?" said Henry, looking behind him to see who the man might be talking to.

"The jerk called me insubordinate," the man spat out. "Prick."

"Some people get mad," said Henry, more to himself than to anyone else. He looked at his shoes.

"Damn right, and I'm not taking any more of his crap, you know?" the stranger said. "I'll show him insubordinate."

"It's not good to be mad," thought Henry out loud, and the stranger continued, "You said it, man. Who does he think he is, anyway? I should have punched him out."

Henry kept silent.

The stranger slammed a plastic lid over his chili. "Good talking to you, man," he said to Henry. "You understand what I'm saying. See you around." He slapped Henry's shoulder again, this time in camaraderie, and walked away.

"Bye bye," said Henry. He was glad to see the guy go.

Henry decided on some chicken noodle soup and a hard roll. There were two more houses to shovel out this afternoon, he reminded himself. Henry doesn't come cheap but he does a good job. He always asks the owner of the house to come out and tell him if his work is acceptable before he goes on to his next job. Once an Aspen company called Lance the Landscaper and Snow Removal Company LLC tried to expand its operation to Switchback, but no one ever called the number they advertised in *The Tailings*. No landscape corporation is going to have a glass of lemonade on your front porch after cutting your grass. No landscape corporation has a dog that sits at your gate till the job is done, wagging its enormous tail. You don't feel so good about having a chat with a landscape company. Those guys are in such a hurry. They tell you how much to make the check out for, and they load up their noisy machines back on the truck, and you're glad when they're gone.

SECOND CHANCE

I am a traveler in time.

--Norman Sanger

"Sorry I'm late," said Katie to Thea as she shook the snow from her coat. "There was another accident in the canyon. At least I was on the bus, and not sitting in my own car burning up gas. I got to do a crossword puzzle and read the personals."

"Actually, you're the first one here," said Thea. "Barb called half an hour ago. She's waiting for someone to come and give her car a jump. It wouldn't start this morning. Pour yourself a cup of coffee. How's life in Switchback these days? Met anybody?"

Katie took a noisy sip. "I'm still meeting the neighbors. They come by to tell me what they didn't like about the last woman who lived in my house. Just in case I'm thinking of acting up."

"What didn't they like about her?"

"Number one, she had a little dog that yapped all the time. They said they are glad I just have a cat, but they warned me she'd better not chase away any of the birds from their feeders."

"What else?"

"She planted yarrow."

"What's yarrow?"

"I think it's a weed. It's pretty, though. The lady down the street has it growing on her berm, and everyone says she's got the nicest garden in town. Of course, you can't see it now, for all the snow. But in the summer, people stop their cars and take pictures of it."

"Yarrow. Berms. Boring," said Thea.

"It's not so bad," Katie said. "Everyone has a story they want to tell."

"How's Eric? Is he coming home for Thanksgiving?"

"No. The plane ticket is too expensive. He's going to my mom's."

"And you? Have you met anyone yet? A man?"

"No. I'm enjoying being alone."

"Please," said Thea. "It's not nice to lie to your boss."

"Well, there is this guy who lives down the block. He's kind of cute, I guess. He wears glasses and tie dye headbands. So I figure we have things in common, maybe."

"You don't wear glasses and tie dye."

"No, but he looks like an old hippie. Reminds me of my hitchhiking days. Really, though. I'm not looking for anyone. I'm quite happy on my own."

"Oh, yeah, sure you are," said Thea.

"What I really like is the town itself. It reminds me of the place I grew up," Katie said.

"How's that?"

"Little houses. Families. It's not like *this* place," Katie said, looking outside at the streets of Aspen. "It's *lived* in. In Switchback, I walk home from the bus stop at night and there are lights in all the windows. You can see people making dinner, watching TV. People are *home.*"

"That must be strange," Thea said. "Keith and I are the only ones who live on our block anymore. Except for holidays, we hardly see a neighbor all season. No one lives in our neighborhood. They just *own* in our neighborhood and come out for a few days over the holidays."

"And the people who work here have to move away because there's no place left that a worker bee can afford," said Katie.

"So they move to Switchback," Thea said. "Cheaper."

"Yeah. Anyway, sometimes that town is like a dream of my childhood. Like having a second chance at it."

"That would be nice," Thea said. "In some ways, at least."

"Can I read you something?" Katie said. "I wrote this on the bus this morning:"

Sometimes you have to go back to that last spot where your life was good, the time right before you faced that thing that knocked you for a loop. You have to place yourself back in a time where things were still OK. If you can go back physically to that sweet place, you're lucky. It will be easier. But sometimes the actual, physical place isn't there anymore. The old house burned down or the neighborhood was razed, or the parent with whom you want to reconcile is dead. So you have to get back there another way, and you have to invent the way yourself.

"I had a therapist who talked about that," said Thea. "She tried to get me to do this meditation to go back to the time right before that creep broke into my apartment in Denver. I had to imagine what I did that day before it happened. It actually felt like I was living it over again, only now I could handle it better. At first, I was afraid to take myself back, even in my mind. I cried. I didn't want to go."

"Sometimes it takes real effort," Katie agreed. "It's hard to put yourself back in time, even when your memories are good. But in Switchback, I don't even have to try. It just happens."

Barb arrived, removing her fur hat and shaking her shiny red hair. "Like when I smell chicken frying and I'm back in my grandma's kitchen. Not that I'd touch the stuff anymore with all those calories."

"Ironing is what does it to me," said Thea. "The smell of it makes me feel safe. My mom used to iron while I took my nap."

"How about sound of a baseball game on the radio in the summer?" added Charlotte, setting her latte on the counter before removing her black Armani coat. "It makes me feel like a little kid."

Katie nodded. "That's what I'm talking about. For instance, in Switchback the sidewalks have cracks in them. We don't have perfect sidewalks like they do in resort towns where they're afraid some tourist will trip and sue the city. The other day I stepped carefully over a crack in the concrete and zap! there I was, seven years old again, hop scotching to school the day before Mrs. Tyrrel told my mother I was disruptive. I snorted during the pledge of allegiance," she explained.

"You're *still* disruptive," Barb said.

"They say that once you position yourself again on the threshold of that bad day, you can go through it with more strength the second time," Thea said .

"But you will only be going through it in your mind," said Barb. "Not for real."

"That's the way we go through everything," Katie said . "In our minds. Our minds are very real."

"Maybe it's like taking a test over and over again until you pass," said Thea. "Each time, you learn a little something that helps you do better the next time around."

"I hate tests," said Barb. "I was a terrible student. The only test I ever passed was the home pregnancy one. A-plus, every time. I had a four-point O average in fertility."

"I always like multiple choice best," said Thea, who was on her third marriage. "Which do you choose, husband a, b, c or d?"

"D being none of the above?" asked Katie. "Then I pick D."

"No, D being Door, which we'd better open. It's nine-thirty, and footwear is half off today. Who can resist this place during a shoe sale?

GERTIE'S REVENGE

*Beliefs last because they are founded on things be-
yond the powers of reason to deal with them.*
--Norman Sanger

Eight hundred miles southwest of Switchback, in
Palm Springs, California, a doorbell rings. No one is there.
The electrician comes over. He says that nothing seems to
be wrong. He tells Valerie to call him when the doorbell is
actually *ringing*, not after. Now he's gone and it's started
up again. She stands on the porch and watches it as it rings.
Ding ding ding ding ding. The noise stops when she
reaches for the phone to dial the electrician's number again.
Must be some kind of short. Must have something to do
with the garage door opener or the new air conditioning
system. What a pain. Maybe she should just have him take
the bell out completely and get one of those door knockers
like in the old days. But if that went off too…

She doesn't want to think about it. She shuts the door
and goes back to wrapping Christmas presents. Even after
all these years in California, it seems weird to have flowers
growing in the back yard in December.

On her patio two days later, Valerie read the an-
nouncement of Gertie Howard's death in the on-line ver-

sion of *The Tailings*. Her son, Adam, home for break, gave her his old laptop computer and just last weekend he instructed her in using the Internet. She had hardly slept since then, exploring cyberspace in search of a recipe for tiramisu, the weather in Rome, the words for Mack the Knife. She found what she thought was an old boyfriend, but then, Gregory Kopka is a common name. Isn't it? You never know, though. Not that she'd ever write to him. But she jotted down his e mail address anyway, wondering if he would recognize her with blonde hair. Then she happened upon *The Tailings* website. There on the screen was Gertie. Even though the picture was in black and white, Valerie could see the pink froth of Gertie's hair as vividly as if it had been color television.

She e-mailed her sister, Belinda. *Arriving Switchback tomorrow late. Val.* It sounded like a telegram. Terse. Urgent. The computer made her edgy, made her feel like there was a rush to get somewhere. With her words flying through cyberspace at the speed of light, she felt like she wasn't moving fast enough. She threw a few things in her suitcase, kissed her husband goodbye and pointed the Acura toward the Great Divide, hoping McBain Pass would be open this time of year. Nothing sounded as good as the cozy attic bedroom in her old Colorado house.

—

"You didn't really come back for Gertie's funeral," said Belinda, surprised at her sister's sudden appearance. They looked out Belinda's living room window, across the street at the brick house, where even now some young, unfamiliar visitors were parking in the drive and carrying covered plastic dishes through the snow to the back door.

"I had to," Valerie said. "Stephie and I were really mean to her when we were little. It was after you went away to college. You weren't around."

"Mean? What did you do to her?" Belinda asked.

"We used to play Ding Dong Ditch on her," said Valerie.

Belinda looked across the table at tall, sophisticated Valerie, who she still thought of as her little sister. "Ding Dong Ditch? What's that?"

"It's when you ring the doorbell and then run away," said Valerie, not quite able to hold in a smile. "And then they open the door and nobody's there and they go and sit down again and then you ring the bell again. We used to watch her from behind Mr. Cameron's shrubs next door."

"Well, I don't think Ding Dong Ditch killed her," said Belinda.

"Still, I feel so bad," said Valerie. "What if she had tripped and fallen on the way to the door? What if she had a heart attack?"

"But she didn't. She lived to be ninety-four. Actually, though, she *was* getting up to answer the door when it happened."

"To answer the door?" Valerie said, panic showing in her face.

"The mailman had a package she had to sign for. She got her high blood pressure medicine through the mail. He rang the bell and yelled her name, and then she got up out of her chair and tripped on a rug in the hallway and just fell over. So he ran over and got Mr. Cameron and they broke in the screen door. She's the only person in town who locked her doors, I think."

"She had high blood pressure? Did she have it all her life?"

"I don't know. I suppose so."

"Do you think Stephie and I gave her high blood pressure?"

"I don't think you can give someone high blood pressure," said Belinda, the practical one.

"Maybe she died because she thought it was Stephie and me playing Ding Dong Ditch again and she got so mad she broke a blood vessel or something. I mean, you never know. Old people, they wake up one morning and they think it's 1960, and the doorbell rings and they think it's the mean kids down the block again, even though those kids are forty years old now. I still feel sorry. I always thought I should apologize to her," said Valerie. "We were so mean."

"You weren't mean. You were just kids."

"You wouldn't do anything like that," Valerie said. Her big sister didn't get into trouble, not like she did. "You were the good one. You were always helping everyone. You were the sweetheart of Switchback."

Belinda nodded. It was true. She was the good daughter and Valerie was the troublemaker. Valerie was banned from her junior high graduation ceremony because she and her friends sprayed shaving cream inside Mrs. Poole's desk drawer. "She was a bitch," said Valerie and their parents were shocked. Their mother thought she wouldn't be allowed to go to high school; she would have to get a job bussing tables at the Diner. She would marry a dropout and have twins right off and they would live in the abandoned Chamber of Commerce trailer out on the highway.

"I already had three dozen yellow roses sent to her. Remember Gertie's roses?" asked Valerie hopefully.

"No," said Belinda. "I just remember her yelling at kids all the time. I brought a rum cake over last night." She nodded across the street at the tidy cottage. "It's sure going to be quiet around her from now on," she said, surprised at the sadness she felt.

Switchback has old people of such grace and heroism that they can only be called legends. Gertie Howard, on the other hand, is not a legend to most people in Switchback, although she lived in town at least forty years, in the tidy brick house between Second and Third on Plato Avenue. Walking by Gertie's, you looked in her front door and saw the dim blue light of the television and then you noticed the back of Gertie's very red head as she sat in her favorite chair and watched Jeopardy. Gertie shouted at the television set. "Who was Douglas Fairbanks?" she yelled. "What is the Kremlin?" Gertie was already a widow when she arrived in Switchback, and perhaps it was the fiery red hair that gave her the reputation of being a frightening and wild-tempered woman. No one would dream of asking how her husband passed away; it was impolite. But secretly around their kitchen tables people speculated that Gertie had driven her husband mad and he died a mercifully early death, going to a place that was, finally, quiet. Compared to life with Gertie, that could have been practically anywhere else.

Gertie spent her summers watering the tidy flower beds that surrounded her plain, one-story brick home and grew along the concrete walkway from her front door to the street. The blooms looked so perfect you thought they were fake. It was suspected that Gertie used weed killer liberally. Once the Samuelson's cat spent an afternoon rolling around in Gertie's yard and that night he was so sick, they didn't think he would pull through. He drooled for two days and lost interest in the evening grosbeaks at the bird feeder. The vet said he seemed to have been poisoned by some kind of heavy-duty chemical fertilizer he licked off his coat.

Parents warned their children not to annoy Mrs. Howard. If your mother heard Gertie yelling at you from the kitchen window where she was doing the lunch dishes, there would be hell to pay when you came home for supper. The truth was that moms themselves had been yelled at by Gertie and no one, no matter how easy-going, has ever endured one of Gertie's tongue lashings and volunteered to go back for more. Kids learned early that if Gertie yelled at you and your mom found out about it, she'd yell at you next, and then to drive the message home, Gertie would yell at your mom, which would make you feel very, very bad. You might as well just steer clear of Gertie's yard and go to the playground and watch the sixth grade boys give each other bloody noses. It was more peaceful there.

So Gertie was not exactly an honored Switchback person, just an old lady who still got her hair curled and colored once a week. No one could possibly have that shade of hair naturally. She had outlived every hairdresser she'd ever had except for Tundra, a 23-year-old stylist at The Hair And Now Beauty Parlor, who this week sported a spiky lilac-colored hairdo and had a silver plug in her lower lip the size of a pea. "Make it real bright, girlie," said Gertie, and Tundra did. There is no object in nature with with which to compare the color of Gertie's hair. In her final years, Gertie resembled nothing so much as a prune topped with a froth of pink cotton candy, an effect that might be likely to scare babies, but when you have lived around Gertie as long as most people in Switchback, well, you can get used to almost anything.

Even when a person is not terribly admired, when she dies in a small town like Switchback, people show up to see her off, especially if a light lunch is served. The counter in Gertie's kitchen offered sliced meats, rolls, carrot salad, potato salad, and just plain salad. Christmas cookies were represented in abundance. Everyone was there, including the old folks. Even Oscar came from down the street. He doesn't do much anymore, but he still lives at home, alone. Oscar sits in his living room window every morning from 6:30 until the Meals on Wheels van arrives, leaning over his tape recorder, listening to sermons. Sometimes Oscar stands up, an activity that takes a couple of minutes--and walks outside to his porch to watch the preschool kids go by on their way to Wilson Park. They wave at him. He waves back. That's plenty, when you're one hundred, which Oscar is. Oscar can still recite to you the poem he read to his wife on their wedding day, when he was twenty years old and a sheep rancher up the Ruby River.

Valerie's three dozen yellow roses were by far the biggest arrangement delivered that day. It was so large they had to set it on the floor in front of the fireplace. Valerie thought of Gertie's well-fertilized roses, and she wiped a tear from her eye.

People in Switchback generally think that cut flowers are extravagant and even if it's a funeral, they bring food instead. They will argue that when you live in a place where brilliant bluebells grow wild in the alleys, where columbines of unbelievable delicacy cover the high meadows just outside of town, nothing you can buy is quite so beautiful. A man courting a woman may pick a bunch of Shasta daisies on the walk leading up to her house, but he probably also carries a plate of cupcakes or at least a bag of chips, just to cover all the bases. In Switchback they think flowers look best in their place of growing, and if you really like someone, you should take them up to McBain Pass some summer day and walk through a field of Indian paintbrush with them, never picking a one. Even in the winter, store-bought flowers are rarely seen.

Valerie made herself a turkey sandwich and joined Belinda, who was sitting in the corner of Gertie's living room, staring outside at the snow-covered yard. "You know," said Valerie, "I've never been inside this house before. I always thought it would be creepy and dark. But it's just a regular old-lady's house, with doilies and knick knacks. No poison apples or anything."

No one seemed surprised that Valerie had driven eight hundred miles for the funeral. Valerie, like her sister Belinda, was *from* here. Plus, to drive eight hundred miles to visit is no big deal anymore, when you can do it in a day on Interstate 15 in the comfort of your luxurious car, listening to recorded book. This is the modern world. Residents of Switchback drive to Las Vegas at the drop of a hat just like any other red-blooded Americans these days. You can leave your house after breakfast and be on the Strip in time for the $7.99 all-you-can-eat prime rib dinner, if you don't get sidetracked in Utah by the House In The Rock or the solid gold statue of the prophet Moroni.

The sisters sat quietly, watching Gertie's relatives in the kitchen. A pair of redheaded boys reached up and snatched cookies from the platter on the counter, knocking a basket of potato chips onto the linoleum. "Luke! Matt! Don't be such a nuisance! Go outside and play!" and in a flash they were off, slamming the kitchen door, forgetting their hats and mittens, free at last.

"The mom looks so young," said Valerie. "She doesn't look much older than Adam, but look, she has kids already."

"Those boys are Gertie's great-grandchildren," Belinda said. "They were here last Christmas. Their mom is Gertie's granddaughter."

"I didn't know Gertie had kids."

"No one did. I guess she had a daughter when she was pretty young, and she was already grown up when Gertie came to Switchback."

Valerie watched as the mother and another woman looked her way and put their heads together. They wiped their hands on their aprons and approached her.

"Ma'am?" said one. "You wouldn't be Valerie, would you?"

"Yes."

"That was such a beautiful bouquet you sent Grandma. You must have really been good friends."

"It's just that I was such a ..." Valerie choked. "It's just that she was such a good person." Her eyes started to tear up again. Even when she was a child, her eyes watered when she told a lie.

Tundra plopped herself down cross-legged on the floor next to Belinda. "I was her hairdresser," she said. "They wanted me to come and fluff it up for the wake, but I told them she just got it done the day before. Strawberry meringue tint and all. All they had to do was tease it and spray the hell out of it."

"You probably knew her as well as anybody," remarked Belinda.

"All I know is that she was always bitching about old Mr. Cameron," said Tundra. "You'd a thought he was some kind of sicko. But I was just talking to him over in the corner, and he seems real sweet. He was sad that Gertie never liked him. He even mowed her lawn sometimes and all she did was call him names. He said he never could figure it out."

That's weird," said Valerie. "I thought it was only *children* she didn't like."

"She told him his evil brats made her life a living hell," Tundra replied. "But he didn't have kids, he said. Just him and his wife, and she was in a wheel chair."

Valerie stood up abruptly and walked into the kitchen. "Do you have anything stronger than this rum cake?" she asked Gertie's granddaughter. "Gin?"

The lunch broke up early. In a town like Switchback, you don't hang around a party until the last dog dies. You don't stand there with your arms around some long lost friend, reluctant to part. Your long lost friends live here, too. You'll probably see them tomorrow, at the Valley Forge for breakfast, or on the bench in front of the bookstore. In Switchback, people usually go home at a decent hour.

Valerie and Belinda accepted a plate of surplus cookies and walked back across the street. "Nap time," said Valerie, and she walked unsteadily up the stairs.

She looked around her old room. Charming in a rustic sort of way, but she would never come back here to live. Belinda and Patrick were perfectly welcome to the place. She, Valerie, thanked her lucky stars she'd escaped to California. Nothing ever happened here. No wonder she and her best friend, Stephie, could hardly wait to get their first apartment in Boulder when they graduated from high school

Valerie lay back on her old twin bed. The room looked like it did when she was growing up and Stephie used to come over to spend the night. She turned her head and looked out the window through the frost at Gertie's place. Valerie must have been eight or nine the year she got the Girl Scout flashlight for her birthday. She and Stephie stayed up till midnight and then crawled to the window and shone the light into Gertie's bedroom, right on her wrinkled face. It only took a few seconds for Gertie to wake up and stagger over to the window to peer out. But she was too late. Valerie and Stephie by then were hidden behind the curtain, clutching their sides with laughter, trying not to wake anyone else in the house. Then Gertie went back to bed and Stephie and Valerie did it again, making loop de loops on Gertie's bedroom wall. Maybe Gertie would think it was the ghost of her dead husband, coming back to haunt her for being so mean. They giggled wildly when she shook her fist out the window and said, "Damn brats!" her hair a rag mop of pink tendrils in the moonlight.

The last time Valerie and Stephie woke Gertie was the night before their junior prom. They rang her doorbell and ran off through the yards, but it didn't seem so much fun anymore. They just got interested in other things. Ding Dong Ditch seemed dopey after that.

Valerie shuddered and climbed under the down comforter, pulling it up under her chin. Downstairs, the radio played softly in her sister's kitchen. Just before she closed her eyes, Valerie realized why she had come all this way. She knew, now, what she had to do. At peace, she closed her eyes and slept.

.

"Who did you say you were?" old Mr. Cameron asked. He sure had gotten skinny. He put his nose up to the storm door and peered at her over the top of his glasses. He was holding a newspaper.

"I'm Valerie, from across the street? Belinda's sister?"

"Oh sure. Gladys and Hank's kid."

"Yes, sir."

"How is ol' Hank, anyway?" said Mr. Cameron.

"He died about fifteen years ago, Mr. Cameron," Valerie said.

"You don't say. He sure could flip a steak on that barbecue. How's that little short-haired kid in the sandbox?"

"That was me, Mr. Cameron," said Valerie. "I had the pixie haircut. My sister had pigtails."

"Belinda?"

"Yes."

"Belinda was the sweet one," said Mr. Cameron. "She made me a get well card once."

"Say, Mr. Cameron, could I come in for a minute and talk to you?" asked Valerie. "It's about Gertie Howard."

"Mean old floozy," said the man. He unlocked the storm door. "Take a load off," he said, gesturing toward an upholstered chair in his quiet living room.

"Thanks. Mr. Cameron. I was just wondering...did Gertie Howard have some kind of feud with you? You know, something that made her mad?"

"Never could say. I sure tried hard, though, to be neighborly. Mowed her grass and all. Drove her to the doctor once when she tripped over a bag of fertilizer."

"Then what do you think she was mad about?"

"Don't know. She'd see me over the hedge and yell something like, 'Keep those brats at bay!' but I never knew what she was talking about. I think she thought that some of the neighborhood kids were ours, but of course we had no children. We didn't even have nieces and nephews. After awhile, she wouldn't even talk to me. Just turned around and went in the kitchen. Slammed the door. Once she sprayed me with the hose. Knocked my glasses off."

"Mr. Cameron," Valerie said. "I have a confession to make." she took a long breath.

"Who are you?" said the old man.

"I'm Valerie. From across the street?"

"Are you the nice one?"

"No, I'm the other one," she said. "The short-haired kid in the sandbox."

The old man frowned. "You're old. You're not that nice Belinda."

"I'm Valerie, Mr. Cameron," she repeated. "I came to talk about Gertie Howard."

"Bitchy broad," said Mr. Cameron. "Are you Meals on Wheels? What's for lunch?"

"It's late," said Valerie. "You already had lunch. You had it at Gertie Howard's wake."

"She's dead?"

"I have to go, Mr. Cameron," said Valerie. "It was nice seeing you again."

"Say hi to Hank."

"Whatever."

"He sure can flip a steak."

Except for the holiday music blaring constantly in all the shopping malls, Valerie was glad to be back in California. She joined a couple of chat rooms on the Internet. She bid on a set of Fiestaware on Ebay. Yesterday she got a note from Belinda saying that Gertie's two great grandsons are terrorizing the neighborhood. She caught them throwing snowballs at the cat.

There goes the doorbell again. Ding ding ding ding ding. Valerie doesn't get up to answer it. She knows no one is there.

MULCH

The ideal state is to be happy and in love with life.
Life is a dreary waste without someone to love.
                                                    -- Norman Sanger

Of all the organic gardeners in Switchback--and
there are many--Ron Martinez is the most thorough. He
pees in his compost to give it nitrogen. He talks to his to-
matoes as harvest approaches, calls them by name. And, at
the first sign of spring, Ron mulches everything in sight,
stuffing tree branches, weeds, and grass clippings into a
machine that whines like a chain saw cutting through a tin
shed, only not so quiet. But it's only for a day and people in
Switchback never complain about the sound of mulching,
which is a necessary thing. They do, however, telephone
the police the instant a car alarm goes off, or a party to
which they have not been invited gets too noisy. People in
Switchback have their priorities, like anywhere else.

Ron's house is on the stretch of alley that is considered by many to be the best in town. Alley quality, of
course, is a matter of opinion. Last week, the newly-formed
Alley Beautification Committee visited Ron personally to
suggest that he get rid of all that lawn trash--that's what
they called it--that he stores in piles by his fence. "I'm saving it till I get a real big pile and then I'm going to mulch

it," Ron told them patiently. Ron is much more patient with the Alley Beautification Committee than they are with him. They take photos of his lawn trash and e-mail them to the town manager, as an example of how Switchback needs some stricter laws about tidiness. It's just so unattractive, all those branches, compost piles and empty flowerpots that people put out there, they say among themselves. The town manager telephones Ron and tells him about the complaints, and then he goes over to take a look for himself. "Nice compost," he says, and then they go to the Valley Forge for lunch. In this way Ron and the town manager, who have been friends ever since they shared a joint after painting Ida Contino's house together one weekend years ago, get to have lunch together every two weeks and catch up on old times.

Alleys aren't such a big deal to most people. People who don't have alleys of their own don't give them any more thought than you would the rag man, or the backyard scarecrow, or any other relic that has slipped out of your life and been replaced by progress. Many people, given the choice, pack up and move away from places with alleys to places without them. Now they look out their back doors to other back doors, across expanses of perfect lawn separated by well-fertilized rows of roses or a chain link fence. If they miss the alleys of their youth, they don't know it anymore.

But in Switchback, being old and a coal mining town--at least until the explosion--well, they just didn't know any better; they didn't know about progress. They didn't know that alleys were hopelessly outdated. No one had told them yet that a garage is supposed to be big and well-lit, facing onto the street like an enormous, gaping mouth, its doors rolled up like lips, so you can the new cars inside. No, in Switchback they still think garages are where you do projects. You oil your tools on a bench inside on a rainy day or make a puppet theater for your kids. Progress passed

Switchback by, taking a quick look and declaring it a hopeless case. Progress said, "No, thanks, I'll just go up the road to that subdivision on the golf course," leaving alleys to people too backward to know the difference.

Animals like the alleys, though. The cats come to watch the birds, who eat the insects that hide in the grasses on the banks of the ditch. In addition to the usual house pets, there is the lady on the end of the block with the horse trailer. She has only lived there for three years and no one exactly knows her name, although she told them once but they forgot and now it's been so long it seems impolite to ask again. They should have paid better attention but they didn't think she'd last more than one winter. There is also the parrot who squawks from the apartment over the garage in the big blue house. Oh yes, and one more part-time cat, age fifteen, whose owners moved to the other side of town and took her with them, but Libby keeps trotting back to the vegetable garden where she was born, where she can keep an eye on the chickens, in whom she takes a motherly interest, having known them since they were eggs. Libby is not one of those wandering cats. She never got the urge to move to another place; this garden is just fine, thank you.

The chickens get a lot of attention. People who go for walks after supper usually take the alley route just to look at them. They cluck over the fence at the hens, and chase escapees back into the pen when they fly out and find themselves, confused, in the hollyhocks, staring Libby in the face. No sightseer's tour to Switchback is complete without a visit to the chicken coop. Switchback folks like to play up the town's rustic qualities when their city relatives come to visit. They say, innocently, "Chickens? You mean you don't have *chickens* where you live? Hard to fathom." Sometimes they scratch their chins to show how this perplexes them. Of course, these same citizens of Switchback do not have chickens themselves. They just like to use these particular chickens to prove a point.

The soft clucking coming from the henhouse is all you can hear on some days.

But not if it's the day that Ron drags out his chipper and straps his respirator to his face, giving him the appearance of a giant grasshopper. On that day the screams of his machinery can be heard clear over to Main Street. "Ron's at it again," people say, and some of them bring over some lawn trash of their own to add to the mix.

Katie was still a newcomer to town and not a gardener herself. Her experience with plants was limited to some celery stalks, which she stuck in water to keep them fresh longer in the refrigerator. She planned to spend her sunny days off by catching up on her reading while she waited to see what might pop up once the ground thawed. She didn't know a thistle from a rose, although she thought they were in the same family, both having thorns and all. All last winter, Ron drove past Katie's house on his way to work, and noticed that no other man seemed to be in the picture. So one morning in March, he brought Katie a fifty-five gallon drum of mulch. He heaved it out of the truck and set it next to her gas meter out back. In his worn tie dyed T-shirt, a faded bandana holding down his long hair, Ron looked to Katie like a poet she met long ago at a protest march.

"What's that?" Katie asked.

"It's mulch," said Ron, wiping the sweat from beneath his glasses. "I just made it," he continued proudly, as if he had baked a chocolate cake from scratch, or built a log cabin with his bare hands. Katie poked at it with a finger, as if testing for doneness. "Looks good," she pronounced expertly. Let him think she knew her mulch. Whatever it was. "Thank you very much."

Then she went to see Ann Chadwick, the widow down the street who was known for her vast knowledge of gardening. Ann's expertise was famous as far away as Denver, and every weekend in the summer, Katie had heard said, strangers could be seen taking photographs of her legendary berm.

"That Ron guy gave me a garbage can full of mulch stuff," Katie said to Ann, observing on the kitchen table a collection of mason jars containing various seeds, including one labeled "alley spinach."

"Mulch? That's impossible."

"Why?"

"Mulch is too valuable. Probably what he gave you was compost. He urinates in his compost, you know," said Ann in a whisper. "I saw him."

"Huh?" said Katie. She wiped her finger on her shirt.

"It's good for the compost. I wish I had a man around to pee in mine," Ann defended. "I don't know if his old girlfriend knew what a good thing she had there."

Katie was confused. "I thought he said it was mulch. Would you come take a look for me?"

Together the two women walked back to Katie's house. "There it is," Katie said, indicating the huge plastic container.

Carefully Ann lifted the lid off the garbage can. The golden light from the newly-mulched branches reflected back onto her glasses, making her eyes shine like daffodils.

"Fifty-five gallons of pure mulch," Ann said breathlessly. "This is serious."

"What's serious?" Katie asked .

The widow thought for a moment, taking time to frame her words. "In his world, this is equivalent to dinner out at a fancy restaurant. I had no idea his intentions were this earnest."

A week later, walking through the alley past Ann's back yard on a sunny Sunday afternoon, Katie noticed a circle of women, old friends of Ann's, who called themselves, aptly, The Crones. Like druids, they sat in a circle, and each held a glass of wine in a wrinkled hand. Ann invited her over.

"This is my new neighbor, Katie," Ann said. They peered up at her, blankly.

"She's the one with the mulch."

Every face lit up, appraising the younger woman.

"Ah, the mulch," they crooned in unison. They raised their glasses and toasted her good fortune.

IF ONLY HE HAD A SIGN

To be absolutely sure of anything one must know very little about it. --Norman Sanger

Katie read aloud to Ron Martinez from Norman Sanger's Journal. It was the least she could do, she figured, after he turned over all the dirt in the old garden plot along the fence, instructing her to remove the dandelions to the compost pile he'd started for her out back. Ron took a sip from his beer. "That Norman Sanger fellow sounds like Ned down the block," he said, reaching down to pull a clump of invasive bindweed from the walk. "He knew very little about Switchback. But he moved here anyway. It's a good story."   So he told it.

When he heard the thunk, Ron began, Ned O'Connor swore under his breath. If your car makes that kind of noise, you don't press your luck. You stop. It's a hundred more lonely miles to your so-called swinging bachelor pad in Steamboat Springs. As exotic as it may seem when you are in your twenties, when you reach your forties and your wife has announced she has to leave you in order to live up to her full potential, it doesn't sound like so much fun anymore, bachelorhood. It sounds degenerate. Ned feels too old for partying. "When did party become a verb?" he wonders. He is too tired for what he clearly remembers as the horrors of courtship. He also feels too old to be driving this ancient bucket of bolts, not much better than the wheels he had when he first arrived in Colorado to be a ski bum after college, the year he hung a sign that said "Club Ned" over the door to his bedroom and papered the cheap walls with posters from rock concerts. That was when he was sure of himself. Now, he just wishes someone would tell him what to do. If only he had a sign.

The mechanic on duty at Switchback Automotive looked up as Ned pulled in. "Sounds like a bearing," he said. "I can get to it this afternoon, but I promised a couple of oil changes first. Is six o'clock OK with you?"

"Sure. Whatever," Ned said limply. What's the difference where you are when the sun goes down? It's not like anyone is waiting for you at home.

It was the first warm day of spring in Switchback, the day when the purple and golden crocuses all opened up at once, like a crop of fresh-painted Easter eggs lined up along the post office sidewalk. Water flowed in clear rivulets down the street, fresh from mountain snowmelt. The ornate iron drinking fountain burbled. A golden retriever stood on his back legs and lapped noisily at the water. It made Ned think of Delaware, where he attended first grade and had to stand on his toes to get a drink from the fountain by the town swimming pool. Why think about that now? Maybe it was the liquid sound, or the smell of lilacs about to pop. Maybe it was the fact that his best friend, Scott, had a dog just like this one. What was that dog's name? Yeller?

"Here, Yelpie," a woman's voice called and the retriever loped off.

An old man sitting on a bench looked up at Ned. "What's the password?" he barked. Crazy old bachelor, Ned thought. Bachelor. You don't hear that word so much anymore. It's antiquated. There aren't as many bachelors around as there used to be, but he is one of them now. What does that mean? That he's set in his ways? Available? Homosexual? Ned cringes when someone asks him if his friend, Peter, the town attorney, is gay. Peter has never been married. If you don't have a woman around, Ned has noticed, people start wondering about you. They talk. Will he be the one they talk about next?

Ned read the posters taped to the window of the Novel Idea Bookshop. Yoga Workshop, Room Available for one nonsmoking cat person, Tango Lessons, End Hunger in Central America. Where did people get the energy for all this commitment? he wondered. There was a poster for a group called Second Chance Singles. Just thinking about going to a meeting of something called Second Chance Singles made Ned sweat under the arms. Would they ask him about his divorce? Would he have to stand up and tell them about himself? What was to tell? He didn't want to think about it.

The clerk was on the phone when he stepped inside the bookstore door. She put her hand over the mouthpiece and whispered, "Can I help you?" Ned whispered back, "Philosophy." It had been his major in college. She pointed to a shelf. From philosophy major to deputy assessor to divorced middle aged loner, Ned thought. Hardly an impressive climb up the ladder of success. Nothing that would impress them at Second Chance Singles.

His eyes stopped on a slim green volume tucked between two works by John Donne. It couldn't be. He hadn't seen it for years. It got lost in the move from Dover to Boston years ago. His mother promised they could buy another copy when they got settled, but they looked in all the stores and could never find the book again. *The Tall Book of Make Believe.* He pulled it off the shelf, incredulous.

It was exactly as he remembered it when he unwrapped his Christmas presents the year he was seven. Tall and narrow, with a green cover showing dragons peeking around corners, elves rocking in carved wooden chairs. He smoothed his palm possessively over the old, familiar title. Carefully, almost with reverence, he opened the book. "The All-Day Lollipop," his favorite story. There was Johnny holding the huge lollipop, taller even than he was. Ned turned to a tale called "The Very Mischief." In the familiar illustration, fairies splashed around in a glass pitcher of lemonade while a zebra burst through the wall of the kitchen.

The saleswoman hung up the phone. "Isn't that a sweet book," she said.

"It's been out of print for forty years," Ned said, mystified. "I can't believe you have it. Where did it come from?"

"It showed up in a box of library book sale rejects," she said.

"I've been looking for this book for...forever." said Ned. "I don't know what to say."

"Well, you could say here's ten dollars and seventy-one cents," she said with a smile. "And then you could say see you later, because I want to run across the street and get some lunch before they run out of pepperoni like they did yesterday."

Ned checked his watch. It was hours later than he would have guessed. He looked around almost desperately, feeling rushed. He needed more time. He had the uneasy feeling that he wasn't done yet, that there was something he was forgetting to do. A woman, he thinks, will go to all the shops and when she has finished she'll think there's nothing more to do in a place, but a man is different. A man sees more possibilities. He wants to talk to the guy who is fixing the sidewalk in front of the barbershop. He needs to inspect the brickwork around the saloon windows. He wants to taste the water in the drinking fountain by the post office, even if the last user was a sloppy canine named Yel-pie.

Ned found himself hoping that the mechanic had found something seriously wrong with his car, something that would make it necessary to order parts from Denver. Then Ned would have to spend the night in the little motel he'd driven past on the highway next to the Guns 'n' Jewels Pawn Shop. Tango Lessons began at eight, he remembered. Maybe the bookstore lady would be there. Just thinking about getting back on the highway and driving the two hours to his empty apartment made him sad.

Ned glanced across the street. Ben Franklin. Five and Dime. There it was, next to the cafe. How could he have missed it? He decided he could use a few supplies. Toilet paper, razors, some yellow legal pads to make lists on. He hadn't been in a Ben Franklin store since he was a kid in Orchard Falls. His mother used to buy fabric there, underneath a big, slow-moving ceiling fan. "Never pay more than one dollar per yard," Mrs. O'Hare instructed his big sister, Sally, who was learning to sew on the Singer in the upstairs hall. "For that, you can get a nice piece of gingham or a yard of pretty calico." Out of habit over the years, Ned had kept an eye on the price of cotton yard goods. He watched as it rose from $2.69, to $3.88, and now, he knew, the standard price for a yard of gingham or calico at the mall could be six or seven dollars. He wondered if he could get Sally to make him some curtains for the window in his apartment. Something cheerful, his mother would have said, as if the right window coverings could turn his life around.

Although this Ben Franklin Store had no overhead fan, the floor creaked and smelled of furniture wax. Ned found the razors in the toiletries section and selected a toothbrush, in case he had to spend the night. He got a four-pack of toilet paper and looked around for something else to purchase. He pushed his cart past two redheaded boys who were examining boxes containing snap-together model cars. He thought about the plastic Edsel he glued together all by himself the summer after fifth grade. The steering wheel turned and the tires were real rubber.

A man asked Ned if he knew where the shoe polish was, and although he didn't, he said he'd help him look. When they'd found it, Ned popped the lid off a tin of Midnight Black Shoe Wax, sniffed it, and put it in his cart. He hadn't polished a pair of shoes since his senior prom. These days he just wore sneakers and hiking boots.

Ned found himself humming *Bye Bye Love* before he realized it was playing on the speaker system. The Everly Brothers, Phil and Don. It was a song that came out the year he changed schools, when his dad got the job with the tire company in the next state. Once he heard Miss Roselli humming it while she graded papers during recess. The girls sang it on the playground swings, their dresses blowing up over their faces, showing petticoats underneath.

Ned pushed his cart slowly up the aisle. Hair dressing and bubble bath. Craft supplies, Styrofoam balls like his mom used to make Christmas ornaments out of, and decals with cherries and black swans on them. A sheet of fake tattoos, to put on the back of your hand with a moistened sponge. If you were careful, they would last till you had to wash your hands for supper. He found himself under a sign that read FABRICS. There were checks and calicos and something that reminded him of the pajamas he wore when he was sick with the chicken pox. It had brown wagon wheels on it. A sign read: *Nothing over $1 a yard.*

Ned became dizzy, like he'd been spinning too long, arms outstretched, face looking up at the sky. It was hard to take a deep breath. Maybe he was having a heart attack. But wouldn't he feel some pain? When he looked down at his feet, they seemed too close or something. "Excuse me just a minute. I'll be back," he said to the woman in the red apron at the checkout counter, leaving his cart next to the

Gum One Cent machine by the door. He walked unsteadily to a bench outside and made himself breathe slowly. Woozy, he said out loud. He just felt woozy. He peered at the sun glaring on the window of the laundromat across the street. Everything seemed just slightly the wrong size. The laundromat was too little, like a toy. His legs felt wrong. He was afraid to close his eyes. It made him feel like he was falling, sliding through a culvert, unable to slow himself down.

No one noticed how long Ned sat there. It could have been five minutes or an hour. Eventually, the sunlight readjusted itself for his eyes and the world took on the right size again. "I guess I needed a little air," he said to the checkout clerk as he paid for his purchases.

"Yes, sir," she replied. "I guess we all do, once in awhile. Seems there's never enough of it up here."

Ned found himself in Switchback again only a month later. Something was going on in the park. A grown man dressed as a dandelion was reading a poem into the microphone. Ned bought a yellow T-shirt at a booth and entered the horseshoe contest, coming in third. Someone handed him a beer. At the potluck, he thought he caught a whiff of the perfume his grandmother used to wear. He went back to Ben Franklin and found it on a shelf next to the bobby pins. Blue Waltz. He unscrewed the top and sniffed. Suddenly he remembered the rules for canasta. Grandma, Jenny Olsen and Rose Donnelly around a card table covered with an embroidered cloth, letting him sit under the table and draw pictures on the underside with a crayon, like someone in a cave, handing him a Windmill cookie now and then with a wrinkled hand.

Ned started needing more and more things from the Ben Franklin store, even though it was a two-hour drive from his Steamboat Springs apartment. He brought his purchases back home and set them around his two rooms in an attempt at decorating. A refrigerator magnet saying,

"Greetings from Echo Mountain, Colorado," a package of sweet pea seeds that he tacked to his bulletin board. Always a careful environmentalist, he now found himself filling his tank with gas just to drive to Switchback and pick up some potatoes at the produce stand in the Coop parking lot. It was like being in love, always thinking of excuses to drive by your sweetheart's house just to see if she is there.

It was on one of these trips that that Ned saw the For Sale sign in front of the tiny house on Plato Avenue. The real estate lady said it was an unusual situation. The owner hated it here. A former city dweller, he called Switchback "bovine." He would finance the sale to anyone with half-decent credit. Ned had one check left in his wallet, and he wrote it out for $1000, the deposit, signing the contract before driving home to Steamboat.

Ned's car took its final gasp in October at the Homecoming Car Wash and he donated it to the auto shop class, making them promise they would not return it to him even if they got it running, but would have a raffle or something, give it to a charity. He walks everywhere now except for the summer Sunday concerts in Aspen, and then he catches the bus that picks him up in front of the post office drinking fountain. He tried to drink out of it one hot day recently but the old man on the bench said it's been rusted shut for as long as anyone can remember.

THE CHRONOLOGY OF OBSOLESCENCE

One needs only a single glance to tell where the poor working man lives. --Norman Sanger

"You hold the newspaper. I'll drive," Katie told Violet happily. "Garage sale season again at last!"

"I've never seen you like this," said Violet. "Did you drink too much coffee this morning?"

"No. It's just that my Garage Sale Depravation Disorder has begun to lift. I feel human again. It's spring. People are unloading their treasures. Now, pick up that newspaper off the floor in front of you. I circled the sales that look good. There are four of them, five if you count the one up the Ruby. Would you hold on to my coffee while I back out of the alley?"

"You have a real system here," remarked Violet. "What do the numbers mean?"

"That's the order we'll hit them in," explained Katie. "First, I look for the yard sales in the old part of town. Maybe we'll find one where someone has lived in a house for thirty, forty years. Like the one I put the circle around in the paper. On Fourth Street. The couple is moving in with their daughter in Florida. I read about it in *The Tailings* on Thursday. They're going to help her run an coffee shop in Sarasota." She pulled up to a stop in front of the house.

"They might have some nice paintings," said Violet, an artist who showed her work in California and New York galleries.

"Just think," said Katie. "Forty years in the same place. That's a long time. Actually, though, I've been in Colorado for half that long already. Ever since I left college."

"Where did you live before you moved up here? I always meant to ask you."

"Little towns. First I went to Goldflake, and then to Aspen, and now I'm here in Switchback."

"But you seem like a city girl," said Violet, who was born in the Bronx.

"I am. I was. Chicago. But once I got off that motorcycle in Goldflake, I was hooked. I looked up at the Ten Mile Range and felt like I was in one of my grandma's paintings of the Old Country. She was from Slovenia. That's part of Yugoslavia."

"You rode a motorcycle?"

"I caught a ride with the Kansas City Outlaws. Remind me to tell you the story sometime. Twenty years ago, but sometimes it doesn't seem like any time at all."

Time. Katie marked the passage of time in her life by observing trends in yard sale merchandise. "You get that way working in a consignment store," she stated. "Stonewashed denim jeans, tight ski jackets, fitted blazers with small armholes, yoked skirts, low-cut cowboy boots, studded belts, stirrup pants," she ticked off on her fingers. "The cream of the crap. I have seen them all come and go," she said. "The chronology of obsolesce, I call it."

"Like last fall when I moved here," she went on. "The most common yard sale item was the wooden clothes drying rack. Every sale had one."

"I did," said Violet. "I could dry a weeks' worth of lingerie on it, on my front porch."

"Lingerie? You have lingerie? Ooh la la. I just have underwear."

"I like the feel of being scampily clad," said Violet.

"Don't you mean scantily?" Katie asked .

"Whatever. Anyway, I dried all my sexy unmentionables on that rack. The mailman got out of his truck and walked my letters right to the front door every laundry day. Too bad he was married."

"They looked so useful, those racks," Katie said, pulling up in front of an old house with balloons out front. "I had to have one. My relationship with my so-called boyfriend had entered the 'Why beat a dead horse?' stage, and even before I moved up here, I found myself buying things I might need if I were to live alone again someday. Personally, speaking as a consignment store professional, I have observed that people buy things for the lives they think they are going to lead, not the lives they are living at the moment."

"Interesting," Violet said, inspecting a lacy black camisole.

"It was one of those 'quit or be fired' terminations," Katie continued, thinking of her last relationship.

Violet looked up. "Which were you?"

Katie seemed not to hear the question. "He was a compulsive shopper. I never knew a man who shopped like he did. I should have taken it as a sign. He was so fussy. Everything had to be perfect. He must have been insecure. Once he said, 'I wonder if anyone likes me enough to come to my funeral when I die.'"

"What did you say to that?" asked Violet.

"I said, 'Just have a garage sale at the wake. Then lots of people will come. *I* will.'"

Violet laughed. "I take it that was the beginning of the end, as they say. When relationships go sour, you have to bite 'em in the butt."

"Don't you mean nip 'em in the bud?"

"Whatever," said Violet. "Do you even know what you're looking for?"

"I need someone who will let me..." began Katie.

"No, I mean *today*. What *stuff?*"

"Oh. Something cute for the house. Something I've never seen before," mused Katie. She pulled some bills out of the pocket of her jeans and counted them out. "Something under four dollars."

"That's what we all want," said Violet. "Say, were you around for the toy windmills? Every yard sale used to have them."

"No. That must have been before I arrived," Katie said.

"I got mine for fifty cents. It was a work of art...a faithful tin model of a working windmill, complete with a metal ladder up the side. It spun around in the breeze like the real thing."

"Wow. Wish I had one for my yard," said Katie enviously. "I wonder how they all ended up in Switchback."

"I always imagined a door to door windmill salesman selling them out of a suitcase. Maybe he made them in his garage. You know these old guys. Real tinkerers," Violet said with admiration. "Or maybe it was some kind of Boy Scout project, a fund raiser. No one could tell me. All I know is, you saw them all over. You still see them. If you ever wake up one morning and don't know what town you're in, just look around and if you see a tin windmill in a backyard, you're in Switchback, Colorado. You can bet on it."

The women walked past a card table offering dusty old Mason jars for sale. Violet snorted. "They must think we're real suckers," she said. Real locals know that it is futile in Switchback to try and sell canning jars at your yard sale. Maybe if you're lucky you can give some away, but asking money for them is a sign of greed, or, at the very least, naiveté. The abundance of Mason jars comes from living in a climate that, although chilly, offers a wealth of locally-grown food, much of it wild. There are chokecherries for syrup and preserves. There's rhubarb, planted back when the coal mine was still in business. It grows behind sheds, hearty and weather resistant, returning every year, free for the taking. Not to mention the apple trees in almost every back yard, and the wild raspberry bushes along the Ruby Road.

But if you still think you might need an extra case of canning jars, just wait until four in the afternoon and drive by that same yard sale again. "Take them! They're free! Just get them out of here!" the woman will shout as you drive slowly by. She might even pick up a whole case of them and run alongside your car. You just have to be willing to hold out, a discipline that is useful to frugal shoppers. People here know that. The concept of instant gratification has not yet taken hold in Switchback, where it takes a bristlecone pine one hundred years to grow to the size of a shrub.

At the huge discount store in Glenwood Springs, they have Mason jars on the shelves right by the checkout counter all summer long, and they rarely sell a single case. The head buyer has noted this in his monthly reports. That's why the jars are right out in front now, where you can see them as you pay for your stuff, a final reminder before you leave the store, and still no one buys them. They would do better to put encyclopedias there, or cat food, but please, no more Mason jars. You can get them free at any yard sale between April and November, but if you check your own backyard shed, you'll see that you probably have enough already.

An hour away in Aspen, the antique buyers get to yard sales early, wait in their Range Rovers drinking latte out of Styrofoam cups. They know that the castoffs of the wealthy are a banquet, and if you're lucky enough to arrive before Billie Sawyer, whose shop is right across from the

Hotel Jerome, well, you might come home with a beautiful linen tablecloth or a Roseville vase. Billie never lets anyone else have a chance. She carries a cardboard carton box on her hip and tosses things in it without even admiring their lovely details. She never backs off and lets you buy that cute little lamp shade that you probably saw first. At Switchback yard sales, on the other hand, there are no early birds. There are more important things to do here, like having your coffee in the garden before the kids wake up or sitting with a cat on your lap reading the paper. Switchback has only one paper, *The Tailings,* and it comes out on Thursdays and if you read good and slow and do the crossword puzzle, you can make it last till the following issue hits the stands. Of course, it's hard to pace yourself. You want to go right to the Police Blotter and read about the crimes. Last Thursday, everyone read about Mr. Buhler, who was riding his bike down the alley after work and got hit in the chest with a raw egg. The assailant, it was reported, was still at large. This week, a loose lawn mower was apprehended putt-putting down Wilson Avenue without a driver. You just can't be too careful, say the locals. You'd best look both ways before crossing Wilson Avenue from now on. Last summer *The Tailings* carried a story headlined "Big City Crime," about an "alleged graffiti incident" on the fence by the hardware store. Upon closer inspection, the authorities determined that the "graffiti in question" suspiciously resembled a Have a Nice Day Happy Face. Indeed, Pilar Trujillo, an aide at Good Morning Child Care Center, admitted it was her idea for the Friday afternoon art project. "We did it to be nice," she stated, and no charges were pressed.

"You can't call it graffiti when it's a Have a Nice Day Happy Face," said Roland Swanson, the mayor, at the Tuesday night council meeting. Roland is a calm man, not an alarmist, unless you consider his reaction to pesticides on the soccer fields, but that is another story.

Then there's Ned O'Connor, such a nice guy you wonder why he's still alone. If he only knew about all the single women who go to the yard sales in Switchback. Maybe then he'd get up early one Saturday morning and pick through the hand tools in the fifty cent box, strike up a conversation with a nice single lady out buying flowerpots or kitchenware. But Ned is busy with his sweet peas again. Ever since he moved into his cabin on Plato Avenue, he has planted sweet peas. When you do the same thing over and over again, little things dawn on you that help you do it better the next time. The first year, Ned didn't read the directions on the package, and, not a natural gardener, he planted the seeds so deep--some people say it was four to six inches, same as you plant tulips--that they never sprouted. They spent the whole summer deep underground, wondering which way was up. The following spring, he planted the seeds the proper depth, but failed to realize the importance of watering, and although their tiny heads popped out into the sunshine, the flowers never grew more than two inches tall and the edges of their leaves curled up and got crispy before they gave up the ghost. It was such a disappointment to Ned. That was the year he constructed an elaborate system of strings and trellises along his fence. The strings rose four feet into the air and were attached by staples to the tops of the pickets. "They have to have something to climb up," reasoned Ned. Neighbors commented on the network of strings rigged up along the fence, wondering if Ned were some kind of artist. The famous artist, Cristo, as everyone knows, strung a mammoth curtain across a whole valley out near the town of Rifle, and its picture was seen in *Time* magazine and all over the world. Maybe Ned was doing the same thing, only with string. You never knew.

But Belinda and Patrick knew, because they lived next door. They woke up to the crack of a staple gun and looked out their bedroom window to see Ned tacking lengths of sisal cord to his picket fence. "Those sweet peas are only three inches high," yelled Patrick, and Ned explained, "Yeah, but they need something to climb up," and then Patrick went back to bed, but the noise was too much for him and he and Belinda gave up, even though it was a Saturday morning, and they put on their bathrobes and slippers and brought their wooden stools and went over to Ned's to sit and watch him while they drank their coffee.

Belinda and Patrick are becoming more and more like their cats. They are perfectly content sitting still and watching people do things. It is entertaining and it is cheap and, as Belinda will tell you every time you foolishly give her the chance, they do not own a television. How can a person find time to watch some dumb program when there are good books to read? Community work to be done? And how about KSWT, the best FM station in the mountains? Don't they ever turn on the *radio?* Belinda asks them, incredulous.

Just last week, Belinda looked askance at Katie as she handed over a five dollar bill for a black-and-white plastic television set at the annual Sunshine Society Flea Market.

"Do you really need that?" she said with disgust.

But Katie had already dumped the TV in the back seat of her Subaru and was driving off to the next sale, her copy of *The Tailings* folded open to the Classified section, on the dashboard in front of her.

Belinda bought a bundle of gaudy plastic flowers and stuck them in the ground in front of Ned's fence. Maybe those sweet peas just need an example to follow, she would tell him. How do you know what will work until you try it?

DANDELION DAY

Why all this to-do about sun, exercise and fresh air?
--Norman Sanger

Switchback, Colorado, is located near the confluence of two rivers, the Ruby and the Big Falls. One way of picking out the newcomers in town is that they get the names wrong. They call it the "Falls," casually, using it like a nickname. Who would ever call a river, "Falls?" think the people who live there. Falls are falls. But some people are like that. They call you by the nickname they think you ought to have, without checking with you first. If your name is Linda, they call you Lynn. If your name is Susan, they call you Sue, or worse yet, Sooze.

Phillip Hoff is one of the worst, but he doesn't exactly live in Switchback. He is a "part time resident," as he says. He had a house built on the new golf course outside of town, and he comes and goes from his "real" home in Houston. Phillip is the kind of guy who, when you ask him where he lives, he says, "I own a home in Houston, a condo in Park City and a house in Switchback, Colorado. It's outside of Aspen." I guess he didn't hear the question. No one is asking him for net worth. Just the place he calls home.

Phillip never calls anyone by his given name. He latches onto a nickname like a dog with a bone, and consequently, no one knows who he's talking about most of the time. In his attempts to get close to people, an important thing to a man like Phillip, he gets chummy too quickly. It makes people edgy. He calls Mr. Bair, the pharmacist, "Doc." No one calls Mr. Bair "Doc". He calls his good friend, Larry, the retired army colonel, "Poindexter," and no one knows why except Larry himself, who once told an inconsequential story about a private mistaking him for an officer of that name. "How's Poindexter?" Phillip asks Larry's wife, and she says, "Who's Poindexter?" but Phillip persists. He goes into the Wine Kitchen Restaurant and asks the hostess, "Is Poindexter here yet?" and she says, "I don't think so." If Phillip had asked for Larry, the hostess would have pointed him out, sitting at the bar, waiting for Phillip. People in Switchback think Phillip is always talking about strangers, folks they've never met; their attention fades and they remember they have to go back home to turn off the stove or something. They wish he would talk about people they knew, like Mr. Bair the pharmacist, and Linda and Susan and Larry.

Phillip's greatest happiness is being invited to big parties in Aspen and Vail. People usually recognize him; he's tall, athletic and--since he stopped coloring his hair himself--quite dignified. Usually, he brings a camera to these parties. He's a good amateur photographer, and he ends up with pictures showing bright-smiling blondes in ski sweaters and lycra pants, with great dental work and long, red nails. He snaps photos of successful executives and their beautiful wives. In Phillip's snapshots, everyone is smiling their heads off and holding a drink. They are the kind of pictures you see in the society pages of big-city newspapers following a charity ball, only the parties that Phillip attends are just parties, not benefits. Benefits in Aspen and Vail are events you have to buy tickets for. Phillip can't see the sense in buying a ticket for a party when you can go to another one, just as good, for free. Phillip will be the first to admit he's not the bleeding heart type.

The week after Phillip attends a party, he sorts his photographs. Then he calls the people who posed in them and arranges to give them the pictures. He calls the executives and the big-smiling girls. They usually agree to meet him, if only the first time. In that way Phillip finds ski or lunch partners for the day. They may even become friends for a time, until Phillip starts calling Jonathan Rosen "Johnny-o" or "John-John," and Mr. Rosen instructs his assistant to tell Phillip he has left town for the season if he calls one more time.

To hear Phillip talk, you would think he knows a lot of people in Switchback, but who he knows are the people from Houston and Chicago and Aspen who run into each other there. Some of them are his part-time neighbors on the golf course, and others visit Switchback "to take a peek at the mountain folks." They talk about them like they're leprechauns. Switchback citizens can usually predict when the visitors will arrive and they stay home on those days. Sunday brunch at the Valley Forge is a sure bet. In the summer, a bunch of 50-year-olds calling themselves Lawyers on Harleys roar up Evelyn Store Road and announce their arrival with one ear-blasting bellow before cutting the ignition. They read their Wall Street Journals, find other Lawyers on Harleys to breakfast with, and order the Eggs Benedict, which are spectacular. The Valley Forge makes them with fresh hollandaise sauce. You don't have to be an attorney to know they're good.

Phillip and his friends never come to Switchback during the off season. "There's not much to do in that town," they'll tell you. "There's nothing to buy," say their wives, after looking in the windows of the Main Street stores, all of which are closed on weekends. Consequently, they don't know about Dandelion Day.

Dandelion Day started only a few years ago. It began when the town government announced its intent to use pesticides to kill all the dandelions on the soccer fields. Dandelions are so untidy, the new director of the Recreation Board (who lives on the 12th green) informed them. The playing fields were downright yellow with flowers from May till the first frost. It was just so messy, she said. You didn't see dandelions on the *Aspen* soccer fields. You didn't see dandelions on the *golf course*. Lon Hausman, who was on the town council and had the most unnaturally green lawn in town, said he could get a good price on some kind of chemical that would make the dandelions grow so fast they would die of exhaustion within a week.

But Switchback has a solid core of strictly organic gardeners. There are mothers who pick the peas at the peak of their ripeness and strain them for their babies' dinners. There is Ron Martinez, a master gardener, who rings his plants with diatomaceous earth, which irritates the skin of caterpillars so they won't crawl up on the tomato vines. They just slink off, itchy. Ron washes the aphids off his roses by hand and wins the compost competition every year.

These organic gardeners, united in a newly formed Environmental Board, presented their no-pesticide proposal at the next town meeting, and it was accepted. Everyone was invited to meet the following Saturday at the soccer fields, dandelion diggers in hand. Manually, organically, they would remove every last dandelion from the playing field.

Saturday came and went, and everyone had a good time, what with the excellent food and all. In Switchback you can't bring people together without it turning into a potluck. Many dandelions were pulled. And in the process of the pulling, mysteriously, many of the pullers began to feel kindly towards the flowers. They remembered that their grandmothers used to put the young greens in salads.

They tasted old Mr. Popp's dandelion wine, and their hearts warmed. Full-grown adults, full of childlike enchantment, held dandelion blossoms under each other's chins to see if they liked butter. They rolled onto their backs in the grass and pointed out clouds that resembled sheep and angels. On that first magical day of true summer, Dandelion Day came about.

Nowadays Dandelion Day is somewhat more structured, but it retains the spirit of the original party. In the morning, townspeople show up at the park and dig dandelions for a few hours while they catch up on old times. They drink coffee out of a huge urn on the picnic table in the pavilion and eat biscochitos donated by Marta's Convenient Store. People purchase raffle tickets for $1 to win a variety of prizes that are provided by local businesses. Children may exchange a full bag of dug dandelion plants for a free ticket. There is no limit to the number of free tickets they may obtain this way. Sometimes, a generous member of the Environmental Board slips them an extra ticket or two, for their hard work.

At noon is the Dandelion Potluck. Everyone contributes a dish. Last year, the dandelion quiche was the most popular, followed by Ida Contino's dandelion creme pie. This year, it looks like Belinda's tiramisu will take the grand prize. The dandelion brandy that she soaks the ladyfingers in is a nice touch. The Natural Energy Society provides solar ovens which are used to warm the dandelion lasagna and bake the dandelion raisin cookies. As usual, the dandelion granola is the last dish to go, scooped up by the few latecomers who can't pass up a free meal, even if it is green and has the consistency of kitty litter.

After lunch, the mayor reads a proclamation declaring the Dandelion the Town Flower of Switchback, promising that no dandelion on town-owned land will henceforth be poisoned by chemical means.

There is a lot of running around, if you're a kid. There's the Dandelion Toss and the Limbo Contest, and then you check your ticket stubs and see what you've won. Maybe you'll get a bag of golden mulch, donated by Ron Martinez, or an hour of weeding provided by the ten-year old Singer twins. There are no big prizes. In Switchback they remember that many years ago in a nearby ski town, there used to be a local race on St. Patrick's Day called the Pub Crawl. Contestants ran from bar to bar, drinking a shot of Schnapps at each one. The prizes were minimal--a lift ticket, a movie pass, or a box lunch donated by the cafe. Then somebody decided it would be great if United Air Lines would donate a trip for two to Las Vegas, and then a big ski company offered a helicopter tour to the Bugaboos, and an out-of-town stock brokerage firm donated $1000 to the first place winner. Pretty soon, athletes were coming from all over to be in the race. Olympic hopefuls from as far away as Germany showed up. A former third-place winner of the Boston Marathon ran away with the grand prize. It just wasn't the same after they sold out to the big money.

That's Dandelion Day. That's all there is to it. If you are driving past the turnoff some Saturday in April when the fields of Evelyn Store Road are dappled with yellow, that might be the day. Take that old Mexican blanket out of your trunk and spread it out in front of the bandstand, and if you don't have a dandelion puller, we'll let you borrow one of ours.

THE CAT FOOD HEIRESS

"So I'm cutting down on my estrogen," Charlotte said. "I only take it two out of three days now. I'm weaning myself off all pharmaceuticals."

"I could never remember to skip every third day," said Thea.

"You don't have to remember to skip every third day," Charlotte explained patiently. "You just have to *forget* one day in three. It's easy that way."

The take-in room at Theodora's looked like backstage at a high fashion show. It was piled, literally, with sequins and chiffon. All along the back wall, stacked shoulder-height, were boxes of shoes. Armani, Bodega Veneta, Bally. Moving crates the size of small refrigerators filled the back porch.

"Wow. This stuff is luscious. Who brought it in?" asked Katie.

Theodora, her blond hair caught smartly atop her head with a tortoise shell clip, rolled her eyes over toward a petite blonde woman standing in the corner of the room, fondling an alabaster-colored Vera Wang gown, sighing.

"She was my best friend," said the woman in a tiny, Marilyn Monroe voice. She continued to stroke the gown.

"Who?"

"Felina Sanders," Theodora answered. "You know, the pet food heiress."

"I'm just so sad," said the woman. "I am distraught."

"You were friends, Brandi? I didn't know that," Katie said. "I'm so sorry."

"It was so tragic," Brandi said . "That bizarre treadmill accident."

"I read about it in the papers," said Katie. "Poor lady."

"Her family brought all her clothes in *here...a thrift store!*"

"Consignment," Thea corrected flatly.

"They are emptying her beautiful house so they can sell it. Can you imagine?"

"This stuff is absolutely gorgeous," Katie admitted. "Some of the things even have the price tags still on them." She lifted the cuff of an ivory-colored silk blouse. "Yikes. Eight hundred dollars."

Brandi wailed. "She and I were so close," she sobbed, peeking into a shoe box. "Look, the soles aren't even scuffed. Her family is so heartless. So unsentimental."

"Well, it's their decision," said Theodora. "They can always give the money to charity."

"Still, we were so close. Our lockers were right near each other at the club."

"Well, Brandi, we'll get the things priced and put out just as soon as we can. Maybe you'll find something you can remember her by."

Brandi sniffed, taking a tissue out of her fake Chanel pocketbook. "It's so tragic. And she was just.," she sniffed again, "was just..."

"Just what?" asked Katie.

"She was just...my...size."

Later in the day, Thea turned to Katie. "Oh. I forgot to tell you. There was a woman in here who wants to talk to you. Here's her card. Eudora Montblanc. She bought two Louis Vuitton wallets. She read that Dandelion Day piece you wrote for that little newspaper up in Switchback. Here's her card."

"*Western Trends Magazine.* Wow," said Katie. "They're huge."

"She's here doing a story on billionaires' homes. She said to call her at the Hotel Jerome. She wants to talk."

They spent the rest of the day pricing the heiress's wardrobe. Everyone agreed that it was the biggest haul they'd ever gotten at Theodora's. "Look, there's even a brand new wedding dress in here," said Thea.

"She wasn't engaged," Barb said. "She didn't even have a boyfriend."

"That's kind of sad."

"Speaking of boyfriends, how's it going with that Ron guy?" Theodora asked. "He's pretty cute. Ought to tidy up that ponytail, though. He came in here one day looking for you. He brought us garlic."

"Yeah?" Katie smiled. "He's nice. But kind of goofy. Like, last week I was going to have Ann and the crones over for lunch in the garden, and he asked if he could do anything to help. So I asked him to spruce up the yard, you know, wipe off the table and chairs, roll up the hose. Well, half an hour later I look outside and he's not there. The tables and chairs are still all dusty, in the shed."

"Where was he?" asked Barb.

"I call his name...'Ron!'--and he comes out from the side of the house, a pitchfork in his hand, grinning. 'All set!' he says.

'All set? But you haven't even set up the table,' I say.

'Yeah,' he said, 'but the compost is in great shape!' That's what he'd been doing. Turning the stupid compost."

"What did you say?"

"I told him he was goofy," Katie said. "But I invited him to stay and eat. Ann likes him. The two of them took their Chianti out into the yard and weeded until supper was ready. They are both kind of compulsive around crabgrass."

"Well, are you two dating or anything?" Thea asked.

"Isn't that a date?" Katie said. "When you have someone over for supper?"

"No," Barb said, speaking slowly, as if to a child. "A date is when someone takes you to a fancy restaurant and spends a lot of money on you. Don't you read *Cosmo*?"

"I don't like fancy restaurants," Katie said. "I like picnics."

"Then you're goofy, too," said Charlotte. She fingered a sequined dress with a well-manicured hand. "I know better. This time I'm holding out for a rich husband."

"My friend, Ann says that marrying for money is the hardest way to earn it," Katie said. "But, actually, there is this other guy..."

"Another one?" Thea looked up. "In Nowheresville?"

Katie nodded, ignoring the gibe. "He's thoughtful, intelligent and has impossibly high standards. Oh, hell, I guess I should admit it. I think I'm in love."

"In love? What's his name?"

"Norman."

"Norman? Norman what?"

"Norman Sanger. But he's dead. Remember that notebook that came in the box of antiques?"

"Oh, yeah. The old writer-guy."

"Mmmm. Old but sexy. You should have read the piece about holding hands."

"You really had me going for a minute there," said Thea.

"I can hardly wait to get to the part about kissing," said Katie. "I'll bet he likes to take his time. A real connoisseur."

"Sounds like my kind of guy," said Barb. "Smart, sensitive and completely unavailable

FAIR GAME

The will is a power that steadies our civilization--all that is lacking is a better judgment in directing it.
                                        --Norman Sanger

It was after the Fourth of July cookout just a year ago. The Contino men pulled their chairs into the shade of the apricot tree to wait for dessert. If you wanted spectacular fireworks, the Continos believed, you could drive to Aspen and get caught in a two-hour traffic jam, or you could content yourself with a couple of sparklers and an Echo Mountain sunset over your Switchback back yard. Take your pick.

Evening grosbeaks flitted around the bird feeder, fighting for the best position. Every few seconds, they were dive-bombed by gangs of hungry chickadees who by the sheer force of their numbers frightened the larger birds into retreat, scattering seeds all over the place. It was no surprise that the Contino's yard had sunflowers growing everywhere. The birds planted them, and then they saw to it that they were generously fertilized.

A fat gray squirrel leapt from the gutter to the bird feeder, sending grosbeaks flapping in all directions. "Say, Frankie, why don't you make you one of them squirrel-proof feeders?" asked Elmer, his cousin. It wasn't that Elmer cared much for birds, but he was a lover of gadgets. Elmer had a self-turning kitchen waste composter and a solar powered skunk repeller. Elmer kept all his Popular Mechanics magazines stored in chronological order under his workbench. "I could bring you the blueprints for the Squirrel Scammer from the 1998 Spring issue," he offered.

"Naw, Madge kind of likes that squirrel," Frankie said, nodding at his wife of thirty years. "He's been hanging around here for as long as I can remember. We even kept him in the house for a coupla weeks after the cat got ahold of him and bit him in the ear. See that little hole? You could put an earring in it. Not that he'd let you."

"He lived in a shoe box on the floor under our bed," said Madge. "He ate caramel corn right out of my hand. But then he started pulling the stuffing out of the mattress. He took it into the closet and made a nest in Frankie's slipper."

"Here, Squirrley!" she called, setting an ear of sweet corn in the crook of the tree. Squirrley jumped from the bird feeder and claimed his prize. "He likes it with lots of butter and Cajun seasoning," Madge said proudly.

The midsummer sun finally began to drop. Deep, satisfied belches were heard all around. It had been a great cookout. Steaks and hot dogs, and, as a concession to the womenfolk who always seemed to be watching their weight, cut-up vegetables with lite ranch dressing. Madge, as usual, made her Sea Foam Surprise, the Jell-O dish that won her honorable mention at the Potato Day cookoff. In it she substituted half a cup of diced, boiled spuds for the marshmallow bits. "That's the surprise part," she told the judges as she accepted the prize, a brass-plated vegetable peeler.

As the evening shadows grew sharper against the red hills, the talk drifted to the upcoming hunting season.

"I'm gonna rent my cabin out to those guys from California again," Sam said. "It's the easiest money I make all year."

"Jim and I are going down to New Mexico for a change," said another. "We're going to fish the Pecos and meet the wives in Santa Fe when the week's up."

Elmer said the best hunting trip he'd ever had was with his dad in 1943, the fall after he came home from the war in the Pacific. "Pa was so cold," Elmer said. "It'd been two years since he'd seen snow. He kept complaining he was gonna get frostbit but he wore so many pairs of gloves that he couldn't pull the trigger. He finally rigged up a way to pull it back with a sixteen penny nail and a key chain. Never seen anything like it." Elmer belched deeply. "I'm so full I can't hardly eat another one of these brownies, but, Lord, if I had a taste of that venison meat now, I'd think I'd gone to heaven."

The men talked about their autumn plans. George and Jim liked to fish. Wayne preferred grouse hunting. Mike was strictly a bow man, went out all alone before rifle season and usually came back with a buck for the freezer.

It didn't take long that evening before the idea of the wild game dinner was born. It made good sense, with them being descendants of the pioneers and all. The celebratory meal would take place in early November, they decided, each man bringing what he'd bagged in the fall. The women would cook up the elk steaks and salmon filets and venison tacos. A real old-fashioned feast. No more dried-out burgers and hot dogs. This year, they'd eat like their grandfathers used to--good, wild meat, and plenty of it. They'd recount their hunting sagas in every rich detail and the young ones would hang on every word, eager for the day that they, too, could participate in the ancient chase. It would be like the old days again, if only once a year at the Contino Family Game Dinner.

You couldn't stop for a package of hooks at Sportsman's Surplus without getting drawn into a conversation about the upcoming feast. "Mike Contino bought one of these scopes just last week," said the salesman. "He's going hunting up on the Flat Tops."

"I heard. The whole family's going hunting, sounds like. There won't be a Contino man in town all October."

At the market, the women were talking, too. "I found an old recipe for possum in my grandma's cookbook," Gloria said. "Do you think when they say to use sage, they meant store-bought or sagebrush?"

Gear was checked, plans were made. Jim and George camped at the edge of the Pecos Wilderness in New Mexico. By the time they packed their tackle boxes and poles, nets and waders, creels and beer, they decided to set up camp in the parking lot at the trailhead and hike in every day. The second morning out, Jim stepped through the ceiling of a beaver lodge, waking the beaver and spraining his own ankle, but they stayed on until they had the most perfect passel of green-backed cutthroats, iridescent and smoky-tasting. Jim made himself a primitive splint out of a coffee can and some electricians' tape. "Elmer woulda done better," he said as he examined his tin can cast. "But it'll make a good story."

Meanwhile, Elmer and his eldest son fashioned a winch for the jeep out of a US Government Surplus pulley and an anchor chain, but all that iron made the vehicle so front-heavy they couldn't get traction on the uphills. They got out and walked, spotting a herd of elk just below Cyclone Ridge in North Park. Their first shot missed, sending the herd scrambling into the scrub oak, and it took all the next day to sneak up on them again. In the early morning before the sky turned light, they were gently wakened by the conversation of two great horned owls high in an

Engleman spruce. They came home in triumph, dropping the bull elk off at the processor in Kremmling. "Virginia says she won't let it in the house unless it's packaged in Styrofoam trays with plastic wrap over the top like real meat," complained Elmer. "Serves me right for marrying a city woman."

Contino menfolk met on Main Street in front of the liquor store and compared notes. "I'm bringing a wild turkey I chased up Butcher's Creek," bragged one.

Another said, "What I really wanted was to kill was that coyote that got my sheep, but no one but a buzzard would eat a dead coyote. I'm going out for salmon on Grand Mesa later in the season."

Frankie Contino ran into Pete, George's little boy, at the Potato Parade. Pete asked, "Uncle Frankie, what are you bringing to the game dinner? I trapped a rabbit!" Pete was eleven.

"I dunno yet," said Frankie. "I was gonna go out and shoot a deer last month but Madge wanted me to clean out the garage. Then, I had lousy luck on the Ruby last week. The blasting up at the ski area had them fish spooked. I dunno. I'll get something, though. No problem." He absentmindedly patted Pete on the head .

Everyone in town knew how the menu was progressing. There was venison, fowl, even a bear. There was trout, whitefish, salmon and crawdads. In a late-season act of extravagance, Doc Contino flew to Texas to hunt wild boar on a private reserve near Baytown. It cost him more than the down payment on his first house, but he came home with the head, to mount on the wall of his den, plus a cooler full of roasts.

"If the menfolk are going back to the old ways, then we should, too," said Angela. She organized a serviceberry expedition that ended abruptly when they disturbed a wasps' nest in a log. They decided instead to go for rose hips, and Ida gave them instructions on how to prepare the tiny apple-like fruits for jam. Wilma made a pie from the rhubarb she found growing behind the old home place, untended for thirty years. No one knew how they were going to eat it all.

Old man Spivak, down off the hill to pick up his mail, asked Frankie, "Did you get anything yet? Time's getting short." Old man Spivak usually couldn't remember his own name. But he was sharp enough to know that Frankie hadn't yet caught anything for his family game dinner. "Naw, I'm waiting till it snows. It's easier to track 'em," Frankie answered.

"I got some ground turkey in the freezer," said Spivak. "Tastes like rabbit. Just put some juniper berries in it. Fools 'em every time."

"No thanks. I'll get something. There's still a couple of weeks."

If he hadn't had his mind on the elk tracks leading into the aspen grove, Frankie might have given more thought to the place he parked his car. He cut the engine and grabbed his rifle, following the fresh prints. It took a moment before his ears recognized the low rumble that came just after he took aim...and missed. The avalanche slid hissing right into the passenger's door and clear over the roof, leaving only the tip of the radio antenna exposed. It would be June before he stood a chance of winching it out. Luckily, or maybe not, a bunch of tourists chose that moment to roar by on their snowmobiles, and it was only after he let them take his picture next to the scene of the disaster that they agreed to give him a lift back to town. "Wait'll we show this to the gang back home," they laughed.

"Any luck?" Madge asked when Frankie came in the back door.

"Yes. I'm not dead," he said, going out to the garage to drink his beer in peace.

The big day arrived. The hunters dropped their prey off early in the morning at Madge's, where the women were bustling about the kitchen in aprons. They had brought all their cookbooks in order to be prepared for any eventuality, and Ida sat enthroned on a bar stool, shouting out practical advice. "Cook it up with some onions!" she'd order, pointing with a wooden spoon. "Soak it in buttermilk!" Having prepared every kind of wild game in her day, Ida was a veritable volume of culinary wisdom. They marinated, they sautéed, they grilled and broiled. Neighbors walked by and sniffed the air. "It won't be easy going home tonight to meat loaf," they said, sniffing the aroma of garlic and roast meat that wafted out of Marge's kitchen window.

Even Frankie finally presented his catch, some pieces of dark meat marinating in a thick, aromatic Worcestershire sauce. "Here, put this in the pot," he said before he went down to Main Street for a beer with Father Tony.

They had to set up three long tables borrowed from St. Teresa's Senior Lunch Program for all the diners. The platters were laid out on the buffet, and Sage, Madge and Frankie's granddaughter who was going to be an artist when she grew up, hand-lettered the name of every hunter next to his contribution.

The magnificent meal was dished up, and someone said grace. Platters were piled high with every kind of wild game imaginable. Then, one by one, going around the table, the hunters told the stories of their catch. "You wouldn't believe how those wild boars can run," Doc began, gesturing in the air with a piece of meat impaled on his fork. "They take off into the low bushes and you can hear 'em in there, snorting at you. Did you know the males grow a thick shield of skin that's tough enough to stop a bullet? I was lucky I got out of there alive."

"Yeah, well, Jim caught these here cutthroats with his ankle swollen to the size of a tree trunk," George said. "He had to sit with his foot in the stream till his toes about froze off. I had to carry him to the car afterwards, prop his foot up on the dashboard."

"Frankie, it's your turn. What's this stew made of?"

"Nothin'," said Frankie. "It ain't much of a story."

"It's your turn, Frankie," said one of the guys. "We want to hear about it."

"I'll tell you later," mumbled Frankie, shoving a forkful of barbecued venison into his mouth. "Can't talk with my mouth full."

So they continued around the table, each sportsman reciting the carefully-rehearsed tale of his adventure.

"OK, Frankie, you're the last one. Time to tell us the story."

"It doesn't have to be a big story, sweetie," Madge coaxed gently. She used to be a school teacher and was very patient with shy third graders who didn't want to speak up for Show and Tell.

"What is it anyway?" Jim said. "Looks like muskrat stew. Did you bag a muskrat, Frankie?"

"Naw."

"It isn't a woodchuck, is it? Too stringy. Tastes like squirrel."

Madge turned the color of cream gravy. "Frankie," she leaned over to whisper, "you didn't..."

"Sssh," said Frankie.

"Frankie," she said, her voice trembling. "You mean *you shot Squirrley?*"

The look that Frankie gave his wife left no question in the minds of the other menfolk. He had been betrayed. He set down his fork and left the house, looking neither to the right nor to the left, and the next time anyone saw him was Midnight Mass on Christmas Eve sitting next to Madge, who, on this holy day, was still struggling with the concept of forgiveness. The story had gone around Switchback half a dozen times by then so most people had learned to tell it without falling on the floor and hurting themselves laughing. At the tavern now, they changed the menu to read "Squirrley Paws" instead of "Buffalo Wings," and if you order a plate, someone tells the story again, in case you haven't heard it lately.

Frankie, he doesn't see what's so funny, he says. He goes ice fishing most weekends since the lake froze over, to get a jump on next year. Just in case.

ANOTHER STORY

"It is useful to stimulate the enjoyment of life through education."   *--Norman Sanger*

Trina took a leave of absence to have her baby. When she first started student teaching at Switchback Elementary, the students still called teachers by their last names. She was Miss Dougherty then, but now she is Mrs. Deckers and the kids call her Trina. It is the new thing. They don't yet call the principal, Mrs. Langston, by her first name, but Trina wouldn't be surprised if that was just around the corner. Times change.

Some of the six-year-olds cried when Trina said she was going away, but they quieted down when she promised to bring the new baby to class as soon as she possibly could, and she told them that she would be back teaching in a while, and by then they would be third graders. Third graders! Third grade didn't sound like soon...it sounded like forever. Tiffany put her hands on her hips and frowned.

Trina's students liked their new teacher, even though she was kind of old and insisted on being called Miss Longo instead of her first name, which they knew was Natalie. Unlike Trina, who grew up on a ranch outside of town, Miss Longo wore dark-colored suits and high-heeled shoes, and spent a lot of time locking things up so they wouldn't be stolen. The children had never seen a ring so full of keys as big as the one Miss Longo dropped into her purse every morning after checking to see that all the doors to her car were securely locked. She even brought in a special cabinet which locked with an additional key, and had the janitor place it next to her desk. In that cabinet, they noted, Miss Longo kept her lunch, her purse and the attendance book. Kyle, an analytical child, tried to point out to Miss Longo that no matter how many things you lock up, you can never lock up that last key or you won't be able to get to the other keys. "So what's the point?" he asked, curious. Kyle was in the Talented and Gifted program and spent afternoons with a special class, where they did more difficult work than the regular first graders, who were still his best friends. He learned interesting things that he brought back to the classroom to share. Last week, for example, he informed them that people in India do not eat meat because they worship a god named Bubba.

To kick off the first full week of school, Miss Longo chose her Milk Unit, something they loved in Baltimore where she used to teach. Miss Longo was big on food groups, and Dairy was her forte. She liked the illustrations on dairy posters, the smooth symmetry of the eggs, the sparkle of milk bottles. On Monday, she read her students a story about Farmer Fred, who kept a cow named Bessie in a pasture. The gist of the story is that farmer Fred feeds Bessie grain and then he milks her and sells the milk to a man who comes around in a big truck and takes it away to get pasteurized. The plot tends to fall apart after that, but somehow the milk ends up in schools where the children drink it with their cookies. Miss Longo showed the class a picture of Farmer Fred's family, clinking their sparkling milk glasses in a cheerful toast. It's not made clear how Farmer Fred pasteurizes his own family's milk, but somehow, presumably, it gets done.

"Maybe they're drinking soy milk," suggested Kyle. "My mom says that cow's milk is full of dangerous hormones that cause irregular growth patterns in adolescents." Miss Longo pursed her lips and flipped the page.

On Wednesday, a gloriously sunny day, they put their lunches in their backpacks and walked up Potato Hill, which begins at the end of Plato Avenue where the elementary school is located. Miss Longo dressed for the occasion, allowing herself a pair of smart gabardine trousers and some decent walking shoes for the occasion, although she still carried her pocketbook tucked securely under her arm, to thwart thieves. One week earlier, she'd called to arrange a visit to the Spivak ranch for the entire class. "We're a beef operation, ma'am," Lucy Spivak said to Miss Longo. "We only have one milk cow anymore." But Miss Longo said that was all they needed. Some of the moms came along, mostly out of curiosity. Not that they wondered about where milk comes from, but they were curious about the Spivaks. No one knew much about them except the other ranchers, and ranchers don't mingle. The citizens who try so hard to integrate the Latinos and Anglos in Switchback ought to start a similar movement to get the old-time ranchers and the newcomers together. It would be a good project for people who are into lost causes.

The Spivaks have been in Switchback for eighty-five years now, quietly feeding their cattle and cultivating their spuds, and all some people think when they drive up to their plateau outside of town is what nice homesites this land would make. The view of Echo Mountain is unobstructed.

"Give me cows any day," said Ron Martinez one morning at the Valley Forge. This got everyone's attention because it is well known that Ron is a vegetarian. "I'd rather see a herd of cattle than a bunch of trophy homes up there."

"It's not that I want to see it *developed*," countered a stylish woman who had overheard him. "I just need one little building site to build a house on. I don't see why they can't sell me *that*." Hearing comments like that, Ron just sighs. Plus, he mistrusts women who use so much spray that their hair doesn't move when they turn their heads.

Up on the ranch, Bert Spivak poured orange juice into his coffee, preoccupied with the speech he was supposed to give to the kids that day. He'd never been called on to perform before, at least not since he had to recite The Blind Men and the Elephant in school half a century ago. All he had to do this time, Miss Longo explained, was to milk the cow and say a few words about dairy farming. "Just be yourself," his wife advised. "They're just children, for goodness sake."

Nevertheless, Bert dug a clean shirt out of his closet and paired it up with a red bandana. He looked a little bit like Farmer Fred, except for his terrified expression. He shifted from one foot to the other while Miss Longo explained once more where milk came from, and then, at her signal, he sat on a three-cornered stool and milked his single cow, squirting the stream of milk loudly into the aluminum bucket. That was all there was to it. The children said thank you and filed outside, where they opened their paper sacks and had lunch in the sun. After they had finished, one of the moms produced twenty-one cardboard cups of ice cream, one for each child.

"Where do you think ice cream comes from, students?" she asked.

"Dairy Creme?" Jonathan said, recognizing the trademark on the lid. Kyle slapped his own forehead with one hand and raised the other, waving it in the air. The teacher pretended not to see.

"Becky?"

Becky thought for a moment. "Cows?" she ventured, and by Miss Longo's smiling face she knew she guessed right. Then they all rolled down the hill that was the Spivaks' front yard. Grandma Spivak watched them from the front porch, their laughs sounding like a gurgling brook during spring runoff.

Friday was another big day. As promised, there was a very special surprise in the elementary school parking lot when they arrived. It was a long, shiny motor home with the word "MILK" painted in huge letters along the side. Miss Longo, beaming with pride, told her students that if they would line up very, very quietly, they could go outside to explore the museum on wheels.

They filed past a mannequin dressed as Farmer Fred. They inspected a huge mural of a farm. There was a picture of a machine where the milk got heated to destroy the harmful bacteria. "No, Becky, not *paralyzed. Pasteurized,*" corrected Miss Longo gently.

Finally, at the far end of the vehicle stood a life-sized posterboard cow with a bulging udder. Every child patted the huge, shiny beast on his way out the back door. Some said, "Bye, Bessie."

"Everyone take out a sheet of paper," directed Miss Longo when they returned to the classroom. "Write your name at the top."

Twenty-one pencils scribbled. Miss Longo sat up straight and spoke clearly, "Where does milk come from? Write it down. Don't say the answer out loud."

When you have quizzes like this early on in your life, you don't get so scared of tests later on. It gives you confidence. Twenty one pencils scratched "cow" on their papers. Twenty-one smiling faces looked up at Miss Longo, proud. They *knew.*

The next week, there was another surprise. Trina came back to visit, her tiny baby boy in her arms. The students were each allowed to stroke his soft head once and touch his tiny hand. They showed her their new bulletin board--titled Where Does Milk Come From?--and Rebecca asked Trina if the baby drank milk, and Trina said, "Yes, *my* milk. " There was a moment of awkward confusion and Ryan raised his hand so abruptly that his glasses fell off, but Miss Longo announced it was time for spelling and Trina left and that was that. It's not such a bad way to end a project, is it, with a few unanswered questions? It makes it more like real life.

Now some people might think that a whole week just to learn where milk comes from is an inordinate amount of time. There are many other important things to learn these days. But Miss Longo takes a personal interest in this particular question because she has recently left a man she'd lived with for five years, who, she swears, did not know where food came from. He would come home and ask, "What's for dinner? " and she'd say, "Ravioli," and he'd reply, "I wanted pot roast." She explained to him that pot roast isn't an instant food; it takes many hours to cook. He wanted it to be like a restaurant, where you order what you want and in fifteen minutes they put it in front of you, whatever it is, fresh from the steam table. He was an airline pilot. Now when she looks back at it, Natalie realizes she should have said "Chicken or beef?" given him a choice every night, and then she could have put it in the microwave like he was used to and shoved the other one in the freezer for another time.

Last weekend in Switchback, working on the KSWT Membership drive, Miss Longo met a man named Ned who somewhat shyly invited her over to dinner at his house. "Miss Longo?" he asked. "Is it okay if I call you Natalie? Would you like to come over to my house on Friday night for supper? It's right down the street, the one with the string on the fence." She accepted and he baked a chicken and a made a green salad, and then they went to the Ruby Theater for the eight o'clock movie. She told Ned about the Milk Unit and he laughed and said he had the very same unit when he was in grade school in Delaware. Then he said he'd come next weekend and put up a shelf in her kitchen, which she mentioned she needed, and when he's finished she will make lunch for the two of them. He hopes there are a few sweet peas left to make her a bouquet. Nothing fancy, just something from his garden.

DRUM CIRCLE

"Live not for oneself. Find work to do."
--Norman Sanger

When Katie got home from visiting her mother in Chicago, she went straight to her desk, her sunglasses pushed up on her head. Outside her dusty window, she watched Ida next door, picking a bouquet of fall chrysanthemums. Opening her journal, she wrote: "I have just returned from my mother's house." She sat and stared at the words for a long time. Just stared.

On the crowded flight back to Denver her head was swimming with what she wanted to say, but there was nothing to write on, not even the back of an old shopping list or a used envelope. She'd looked forward to this moment for hours. Her hand had been itching to write, but now it would not move.

Instead, she began a letter to her sister:

Dear Jill,

I just got back from Mom's, so as usual I'm feeling guilty. Maybe it's a woman thing. Sometimes I feel guilty about not being a perfect mother, and now I feel guilty about not being a nicer daughter to Mom, who gave us all her time and attention when we were growing up.

Is guilt natural, do you think? Is it an instinct? My instinct to procreate has faded now that I'm older. I stopped wanting to have a baby many years ago. And isn't it funny--we always think in terms of babies. We don't think, "Gee, I'd like to have an adolescent around again." No, what we want is that cuddly bundle that loves us more than anything in the world, not the silent creatures who look at us, shocked, like we are unexpected guests in their houses who came in without knocking.

Four days with Mom was plenty, for me and, especially, for her. That's something I realized when I found her sleeping, sitting straight up on the couch, in front of All My Children. She thought I was still at Walgreens's getting toothpaste. I actually got into the house without waking her. That was a first. It was impossible to sneak in any time of day or night when we were growing up. Remember? But this visit, I think Mom was tired out by all the talking she did. She never came up for air. She never stopped. There was no silence as long as mom was awake and I was there to listen.

OK. I know. I am guilty of this myself. When Eric comes home from college or when I call him on the phone, I never seem to shut up. I think I can hold him here with the power of my words. I think that as long as I am talking, he cannot leave. But he always does, waiting for me to finish a sentence and then he politely says, "I really have to go now."

I understand Mom better now, and that comes from being a mother of an adult myself. I am between two generations of adults. How did that happen so soon? How can I have a grown child when I am still a child myself? At least I felt like one in Chicago.

Remember when Grandma was alive and Mom took the bus to visit her every other day at the nursing home? It took up most of her day. If Mom ends up at St. Cecilia's like Grandma did, who would visit her? Once I said, "You know, Ma, I will never be as good a daughter as you were," and she said, "That's okay. You live too far away."

We do. Maybe it's our fault for leaving Chicago. It wasn't that we didn't like our folks. We just went our own ways and built our own lives. I never expected to lose a husband. I assumed that Mom and Dad would keep visiting us, that Eric would have a whole, intact family around as he grew up, and that his father would live a long time. But once she was alone herself, Mom didn't want to go anywhere anymore. She never saw your beautiful house. She never came back to Colorado. She didn't mind being alone on holidays, she told us.

Holidays. That's when I really miss the family thing. A few weeks ago on Thanksgiving, I walked past the Contino house down the block, and it was full of people. That same day, Natalie and Violet and I threw a potluck for all our friends who, like us, are at loose ends during the holidays. We had a good time. But I missed my own true family. Do you?

Damn. I wish Mom lived next door to me like Ida. But she'll never leave that big house where we grew up. I wonder what it's going to be like if it ever gets to be too much for her.

I wonder about it so much that last month I went to the Alzheimer's Unit of the old people's home here. Resurrection Nursing Home, it's called. Can you beat that? My neighbor, Judy, has a mother there. Judy is a drummer. She leads something she calls a Drum Circle. When you think of drummers, at least around here, you think of the hippie kids with dreadlocks and gauzy Indian clothing, but Judy is sixty years old. Her gray hair is frizzy and wild and she wears an apron, like somebody's grandmother. When Judy talks, her mother gazes at her with complete adoration. Does she know Judy is her daughter? Judy says no. Their profiles are identical. Even their hair is similar, gray and dry as straw.

Once a month in the Alzheimer's unit, Judy leads a "musical activity" with the patients. I asked if I could come along. "To help," I promised, but really I was curious. I have always liked old people, probably because of Grandma. I still think about her every day.

I helped the nurses wheel nine women into the activity room. We arranged their chairs in a circle and Judy began to talk. "Nice new hairdo, Paula," she said, and Paula smiled and touched her curls. "How's that ankle today, Claire?" she asked and Claire grunted an answer. Judy called her mother by her first name, Sophie. Sophie did not respond.

Then Judy put on the music and led the ladies in some exercises which they did from their chairs. They raised their hands over their heads and swayed them back and forth. They rocked their heads from one shoulder to the other. They call this exercise? I thought. What happened to walking around the block? What happened to playing with the grandkids? These sure didn't look like the activities I envisioned for my own Golden Years.

Mom was never athletic, was she? Like going out after dark, like driving a car, Mom thought physical activity was dangerous. The perils, she believed, far outweighed the benefits. You and I, we never did sports at all. We probably had one of the few mothers in history who never told her children to go outside and get some exercise. She knew we would do it anyway, and when we did, she would worry that something bad would happen. We might break a bone. We might get hit by a car. "Good mothers worry about their children," she told me once, and now that I am a mother, I find myself feeling guilty if I don't worry *enough*. As if worry is some kind of protector.

I remember one beautiful summer night when I was in junior high, taking a walk alone around the block. On the last stretch, under the stars, with the humid Midwestern air just starting to cool, in our quiet neighborhood, I broke into a run for the last block to our front porch. It felt so good to run. But when I got home, I realized that Mom had been in the upstairs bathroom, on the toilet, where you could see the sidewalk from the window, and she said, "Who were you running away from?" "No one," I said, "I just felt like running."

"A likely story," she said. "Why would anyone feel like running?"

Now that I have lived for most of my life in places where the hills are steep and where people ski and hike, climb and jog, all into old age, I marvel at how long Mom has lasted with so little exercise. Nevertheless, she's healthy and limber. She can reach over her head and down past her knees, and she dances around the kitchen when music plays on the radio. These ladies yesterday, you had to take their hands and clap them together for them. You had to lift their toes so they could tap them on the floor.

After a while, Judy began to recite some verse. She talked rhythmically, nursery rhymes mostly, accentuating the words that fell on the downbeat. "Jack be Nim-ble, Jack be Quick," she said, clapping. She could be a kindergarten teacher; she has that kind of patience. A few old hands and heads moved to the rhythm she set.

But everyone's eyes were on the drums in the corner. Those beautiful wooden drums. I watched the women gaze at them, their hands fluttering in anticipation.

Finally Judy and I passed them out, one to each woman. Judy sat on a stool straddling her own drum and began to play. Together, following the tempo that Judy set, we beat on our own instruments. One-two, One-two. One-two One-two.

I looked over at Claire, her hair a wild white halo, and she looked me right in the eye with a smile, like we shared a secret between us. It was hypnotic. How else can I explain it? We were connected. Soon, every woman was beating deliberately on her own drum. They looked around at each other. They nodded. It was like a communal dance. I thought about all the experience that these women possessed in their lives. Somehow it all went into the drumming. With our separate drums and separate lives, we all made one voice. And the sound of that voice went through my heart and right up into the sky.

I left there thinking Judy was some kind of saint whose miracle I had just witnessed. Somehow, she touched each one of us personally. Paula, Sophie and Claire. And of course, me.

I went to the Alzheimer's Unit thinking I would get a preview of how Mom will be someday. But Mom is a different person and may never even need care. She may end up like her aunt Agnes, who called a cab to take her to the hospital, sat down in a waiting room chair and died, after ironing her aprons and telling Grandma where the envelope with the funeral money was hidden in the basement.

That's the way we want it to be. No illness. No discomfort, and no loss of mind. Maybe we'll be lucky, Mom and you and I. Maybe we all will be safe from Alzheimer's at least.

Trixie, my old cat that died, was like Mom. She had this unvarying routine. She meowed the instant the alarm went off, just to make sure I was awake, and she let me sleep in for five minutes. Then she meowed again till I got out of bed. She ran to the kitchen where she sat while I put on the coffee, and then she ran to the bathroom where I brushed my teeth, and next she stood by her dish to be fed. Every morning the same.

Trixie got better at what she did as the years went by. She was so confident that it put a spring in her step. She seemed proud that she did her job so well.

Mom is like that. She moves easily through the house she has lived in for forty-five years, handling the little emergencies with ease, like the smoke detector that goes off whenever she makes toast.

Remember when Grandma moved from her own house into ours? I was so sad for her. In the city, she walked to the German grocery store every day, chatted with the butcher, walked home and worked on her paintings. Then she moved in with us and Dad drove her in the car whenever she needed to go somewhere, and she never painted a picture again. Her creativity dried up. And in a few years, she went to St. Cecelia's but it was another four or five years before she died, although, as she told me many times, she was certainly ready. I guess she was not ready enough, though, because she kept living. She hung on, sitting in a wheel chair because at some point in time she'd stopped moving around and her hips seized up like rusty machinery.

I have Grandma's paintings all over my cabin. People who see them say they look like the mountains around Switchback. They're surprised to hear they are scenes of Slovenia. I have Grandma's kitchen chairs, too, and I use her old sugar bowl. The wall of my little hallway is covered with pictures of her and all our other relatives, back to the eighteen hundreds. When I look at them I get the feeling I am part of a family as big as the one down the block here in Switchback, the Continos. There are dozens of them.

At Resurrection Nursing Home last month, I saw a woman I met last year at her son's restaurant, where she sat at the next table and told me stories then about how Gino liked to cook when he was a little boy, how she taught him to make ravioli in their kitchen in New Jersey. It was such fun listening to her. Then last month when I saw her in the

Alzheimer's unit, I said, "I know you! You're Gino's mother, aren't you?" and she said, "I don't remember."

Well, I don't remember what the point of this letter was, but here it is anyway. I wish you lived next door and we could have holidays together and tea in the afternoons, and every day we'd tell a different story, never repeating ourselves once.

Love,
Your Sister, Katie

PS: What are you doing for fun? I'm writing stories . It's the perfect hobby. Cheap. And I can do it while I ride the bus to work. It's called multi-tasking.

THE PITCH

"Dandelion Day? Dandelion Day? Oh, yes, that adorable little story about that sweet town. What did you say it's called?"

"Switchback," said Katie, nodding at a customer who had just entered Theodora's Consignment and was headed for the handbag rack.

"Switchback. Perfect," said Eudora Montblanc. They were only talking on the phone, but Katie pictured hennaed hair, blunt cut, a black cashmere top, dark red lips. An impossibly hip professional.

"*Western Trends* is doing a big spread on your cute little Switchback for the Fall issue next year. One of our scouts was there last October during The Potato Bash."

"Do you mean Potato Day?"

"That's it. You all gather round and eat potatoes, right? So healthful. So rural. Simplicity is in now, did you know?"

"It is?" Katie asked.

"So, here's the deal. Eight hundred words, something along the same lines as the Dandelion thing. You get the byline, of course, and your picture on the back page. We'll send out our best photographer. We want quaintness here. Aprons and overalls...country chic. We can talk price later. You'll be pleased. I promise."

"Yes. No," Katie laughed. "Let me think about it. I'll get back to you, okay? I'm at work right now."

"Okay. I know you'll say yes. Just let me know by the end of the week. We want to jump on this. *Western Trends* is on the cutting edge of style, Katie-loo. This could be a shot in the arm for your little cookie stand. We can make a town."

"You can make a town *what?*"

The woman laughed, a low-pitched growl. "Cute. Naiveté is your forte. Promise me you'll never change."

"Naiveté?"

"Seriously, though. We have a huge circulation. We'll put some real swank in Switchback. It could be the next Goldflake."

"That's where I used to live. Goldflake." said Katie.

"Perfect! Then you know what I'm talking about."

THE ANTECHAMBER OF COMMERCE

To have friends is a blessing. One must have some-thing outside of himself.   ---Norman Sanger

The Switchback Chamber of Commerce had received a call from Ms. Montblanc, too, a scratchy message left on their antiquated answering machine.

"Sounds like she thinks we're some kind of hot spot," Betty sniffed.

"She must have meant to call Glenwood Springs," Pat replied. "They have that new wine bar."

"We could send her a brochure," Betty suggested.

"Those things are ten years old. They're mimeo-graphed," for God's sake."

"So? What's changed? Nothing."

It could not have been more true. The answering ma-chine, already second hand when it had been donated to the Switchback Chamber of Commerce, had a Reagan sticker on it. The harvest gold telephone had a dial. More than one antique dealer had offered to replace it with something more modern, if only the ladies would consent.

But even Pat and Betty had to admit that it was the end of the line for the mimeo machine. It had sat in the closet for years, dust sticking to its greasy surface in a layer so thick it looked like fur. "Let's get this piece of junk out of here before the snow flies.

"It weighs a ton," grunted Betty.

It had been fifteen years since the last flyer had been run off on the outdated machine, but the ink was as gooey as if it were yesterday. Anywhere you touched it, you got your fingers grimy. "I sure won't miss this thing," said Pat. "Makes one appreciate a good photocopier, don't you think?"

Still jammed in the antiquated piece of equipment was the last document they'd ever printed. Betty tore at it, read the words and laughed. She wiped tears from her eyes with an ink-stained finger and passed it to Pat. "Remember this?" she asked. "Our first newsletter?"

"A newsletter? Why?" Betty's late husband, Sam, had said at the time. "We already have *The Tailings*."

"This will be different," Betty said. "More chatty. We'll put in that funny saying your brother sent us."

"You mean that Murphy thing?" Sam asked. He reached into his pocket, pulling out his brother's letter. "The Laws of Murphy," he read. "One: Nothing is as easy as it looks. Two: Everything takes longer than you think it will Three: If anything can go wrong, it will."

"Sure," Betty replied. "People will think it's funny."

In preparation for their premiere issue of *Chamber Chat*, Pat and Betty spent weeks gathering local gossip. Ethel Rohde had flushed a bear out of her raspberry patch with the weed eater she got for Mothers' Day. An out-of-work actor was hanging out at the Fry Pan, saying he knew Elizabeth Taylor. The old timers, by observing the rate of skunk cabbage growth, were predicting a spring blizzard to rival the one in 1888, the biggest that Switchback had ever seen.

The mimeograph machine was second hand to begin with, left there by the coal company when they slunk out of town after the explosion. The drum was dented and the feeder was bent, but women in those days expected a certain amount of trouble from their office equipment, not like now. Now, they just order a replacement, or they call in a high school kid to do the complicated stuff. Women in offices thirty years ago had to know how to mend a master stencil with blue repair fluid and run a foot-powered Addressograph machine the size of a Volkswagen. It makes it sound like a long time ago, and maybe it was, come to think of it.

Nothing seemed to go right that day. The mimeograph machine's ink tube sprang a leak, squirting blue liquid onto Pat's miniskirt. A screw flew off and rattled down the heat register. Pat and Betty found themselves covered with grease, and they still couldn't get the machine to spit out one good copy. They talked to it. They yelled at it. Pat, the short-tempered one, kicked it hard and used the name of the Lord in vain. Sensing that they meant business, the machine unstuck itself with such a jolt that Betty cranked the handle right into her bony hip, creating a bruise in the shape of a serving spoon.

Finally, all systems seemed to say go. Giving each other a nod, they raised the tray to start feeding in the sheets of paper.

It was said that the noise could be heard across the highway in the power plant office, even with Paul Harvey's noon show on the radio. There was a crash followed by an otherworldly moan. And then the mimeograph machine ground to a permanent stop, the off-center drum squeezing tightly against the paper feeder, never to be released. One partly-printed copy was jammed in the works, and they read the only words that were printed on it, dead center. *If anything can go wrong, it will.*

Ask most residents of Switchback the directions to the Chamber of Commerce and even today and they'll say, "What? Chamber of Commerce? I don't think we have one."

The building is still there, though, a single-wide modular structure that once housed the coal company office. It's across the highway from the power plant, next to the railroad tracks that once carried coal cars down from the old town of Ruby. It sits well back from the highway between the propane storage lot and Marta's Convenient Store, and its gravel parking lot is perpetually pitted with potholes. Not exactly a prime location for an organization whose purpose it is to attract tourists and businesses to town, but folks in Switchback feel it is best to lay your cards on the table first thing. Wouldn't it be dishonest if they pretended Switchback was hip and thriving? Besides, you don't want to attract the kind of people who are impressed by false appearances. They would just get frustrated and leave with hard feelings later on. Best to get it all out in the open straight off. No one will think badly of you for it. They might even thank you some day.

Tourists who maneuver their cars around the potholes and actually go inside the building are not immediately struck by Chamber's charm or the enthusiasm of its employees. The knotty pine paneling has begun to yellow. The carpet, a shade of avocado green popular thirty years ago, is faded at the center of the room. "What's there to do around here?" visitors ask, and Pat says, "Nothing. Not here." But then, sensing their disappointment, she adds, "You can drive thirty miles up to Ruby. They have an old hotel with a fancy dining room. Or you can go that way towards Aspen." She gestures with her thumb, in a manner that people interpret as: *scram.* Pat and Betty always seem to be trying to get you to *leave* town. Betty hands you a map of the surrounding area and a brochure telling about the hot springs in Glenwood. "Better get going," she warns. "Looks like a storm's coming in. You don't want to get stuck *here*."

Most people who end up at the Chamber of Commerce are lost. They ask directions. They want to know where the golf course is or where they can buy antiques. They want to know if you can drive over McBain Pass in a regular car or if you need four wheel drive.

"Depends," says Pat, ominously.

Sometimes the tourists need a doctor and once someone asked for the coroner.

"Coroner?" Betty shrieked. "Orin's out of town. How about the mayor? Better yet, keep driving. There's a coroner in Eagle County. Orin's just a rancher." She did not seem anxious to hear the details. She thought it impolite to pry.

In larger towns, the coroner is a trained medical professional. He has to do autopsies, like on TV. He solves crimes. But in Switchback, it's just Orin, who has held the post for thirty years. Orin is a cattle man who gets elected every term without opposition because he has a chest freezer in his barn. People in town get squeamish when someone suggests using the walk-in at the Valley Forge as a holding facility for Switchback's recently departed; they prefer to see human remains stored farther out of town, not somewhere they might go for breakfast.

So, when someone in Switchback dies, Orin is called in to pronounce him dead. That's all a coroner had to do in the old days when Orin first took up the profession and he sees no reason to change now. He looks at the body, feels the neck for a pulse, lifts an eyelid and pronounces, "Yep. He's dead." Then if for some reason the body has to be held in Switchback overnight, Orin pops it into his chest freezer, even if it means transferring the surplus ground beef to the fridge in his kitchen.

Not long ago, Mabel Lundquist telephoned Orin while he was watching the Miss America Pageant.

"I'm writing my obituary," she said.

"Why? Are you sick?" said Orin, alarmed.

"No. I feel fine," Mabel said. Orin waited. "Sig wrote his obituary the night before he died. He was fit as a fiddle." Sig had been Mabel's husband for forty-one years. "I just have this feeling."

"So this is it then?" Orin asked.

"I called Vivian and told her what pieces I want her to play at my wake. I left my last will and testament on the dining room table."

"Why are you telling me this?" Orin said.

"You're the coroner. Save yourself a trip. When they find me keeled over on the floor tomorrow morning, just pronounce me dead over the phone. Stay home. There's a storm coming in."

Orin looked out the window. A heavy snow had begun to fall.

He stayed home the next day, rearranging the packages of hamburger in his chest freezer and listening for the telephone, just in case. Mabel put the final touches on her obituary, propped it up with a salt shaker on the kitchen table and woke up the following morning feeling surprised and disappointed. Neither one of them ever spoke of the matter again.

No one was more shocked than Betty and Pat last week when they read in *The Tailings* that the Board of Directors had decided to move the Chamber of Commerce over to Main Street by Potato Day, the last week of September. "It'll be a madhouse," complained Pat. "All those tourists. They'll come in and gab all day."

"They'll ask all those questions," shuddered Betty. "Where to eat, how much real estate is going for. As if we'd know." Although they were invited to stay on, Pat and Betty decided it was time to throw in the towel. It was the end of an era, they reckoned. Betty gave the dial telephone to her nephew to sell on eBay.

The new director is a single mom who just got her degree from the college in Grand Junction. She has modern ideas, which is why they hired her, that and the fact that no one else had exactly applied for the position. She wants to print up a calendar of events, things like Dandelion Day and the Talent Show. She wants to create a Business of the Year Award. Although she doesn't start for a few more weeks, she has already made a poster advertising the Old Timers' Fish Fry and Potluck, using a computer. "Guess she's too good for a typewriter," Pat sniffed. She's thinking of having an annual Shakespeare Festival next summer, like she heard they had here in the old days, something about a distinguished stranger who had everybody convinced he was Richard Burton's buddy or something. Some of the old timers still talk about it.

Pat and Betty tried to tell her she'd be opening a can of worms with the Shakespeare thing, but the new director is a determined woman. She plays bridge with the mayor's wife and wants to throw after-hours mixers at a different business every week. Pat asked her if she knew anything about mimeograph machines, and she replied she had seen one in a museum once, a long time ago.

THE TROUPER

Cling to those friends who have the highest ideals and who have some noble qualities. It will do you good to associate with them.   *--Norman Sanger*

1971. It was Harlan Brown, the owner of the Switch-back Art Gallery, who first noticed the distinguished gray-haired stranger who made his entrance the snowy evening of Harlan's well-advertised "Macrocosm and Microcosm" show. He nodded in silent appreciation at "Stanley's Dream," an eight-foot high canvas showing a monstrous club sandwich with walnuts on it, shells and all. He spent a discreet few seconds before the supple nude that vaguely resembled Harlan's wife, at least from the neck up. Passing into the Microcosm Room, he looked at the miniature art-works, like the minuscule painting of a barn and the small, sentimental etching of a mouse. Macrocosm and Microcosm. It was the title of an article about costume jewelry that Harlan had read in *Western Arts;* he liked the ring of it. It sounded cultured. "God knows we could use a little of that scarce commodity in this godforsaken place," he often said to his wife, Darlene.

Darlene, lovely in a red dirndl, her dark hair held back with a headband, served cheddar cheese and Ritz Crackers. It was all the market had to offer in those days, before you could get brie and kiwi fruit like you can now. She cut celery into finger-length stalks and made a spinach dip, following a recipe on the back of a soup mix package. There was plenty of wine, Mateus and Blue Nun, just like at the fancy Aspen galleries.

Outside, the wind was picking up. People began long conversations, looked like they wanted to settle in for the night. Early winter is not the time of year you look forward to going home and being alone. Luckily you still remember October, which reminds you why you live up here. The blazing reds and yellows of the scrub oak are not yet forgotten. The memory of your last walk in the aspens up behind the high meadow is still fresh in your mind.

Early November, it's dark by six o'clock, and unless you have a warm plate of chili waiting for you at home, you might as well hang out at Macrocosm and Microcosm. Have some more crackers and call it supper. There's safety in numbers here, refuge against the dark shadow of winter. You hear the vehicles drive by on the cold, squeaking snow outside and you pull up the collar of your shirt in an effort to keep your neck warm. Maybe you go next door and buy a pizza, bringing it back to the party where everyone can have a slice. You take care of each other this time of year. Everyone shares.

People filed politely past the paintings, careful not to say anything unkind. They didn't want to seem unappreciative. It would be like going to someone's house for dinner and then complaining about the food. Before Harlan and

Darlene had opened the gallery, Switchback's only art shows took place in the school cafeteria; parents walked around until they found the picture with their child's signature on it, and only then did they stop to take a good, long look. They always made an encouraging comment, hard as it may have been to think of something at the time. They didn't want to embarrass anyone. These same people walked past the art in Harlan's Gallery, murmuring, "Good design," or "I never saw a horse quite that color, but that's not to say it's impossible." Good manners are just as important in small towns as anywhere else, maybe more so.

In an hour it would be dark. If you were home, you would have to stoke the stove and put on a second sweater. If you had company, you might play a game or two of cribbage before drinking a hot cup of tea and turning in. In those days before cable TV, video stores and the Internet, the choices in Switchback were limited, especially this time of year.

Harlan watched the stranger with curiosity. Taller than any other man in the room, he dressed plainly, in a ski parka, blue jeans, a turtleneck and scarf. He moved with a dignity that seemed natural to him. He nodded to Harlan, figuring him to be the owner of the establishment, and accepted a glass of Blue Nun from Darlene. "Rodney Hardwick," he said by way of an introduction, his voice deep and well modulated. By the end of the get-together, he had spoken a few polite words with almost everyone there, and his story, what he'd hinted at, was repeated at most every kitchen table in Switchback the next morning.

"He was a Shakespearean actor," declared Mrs. Poole, the English teacher, visibly impressed.

"He's looking for work as a carpenter," Frankie Contino said. "Has all the tools in his truck." They all agreed he looked like a strong man, who even at his age seemed capable of hefting a stack of two-by-fours onto his shoulder and carrying them up a ladder to the second story.

"He lived in Hollywood," Harlan reported. "Knew all the big shots. Elizabeth Taylor. Sir Lawrence Olivier. Says he plans to stay a spell. Nick down at the Landslide is letting him sleep on a cot in the back room. He might do a poetry reading there, maybe something for the holidays. Maybe some Dylan Thomas. Maybe some Yeats." Harlan dropped the names of the poets like he knew them personally. He pronounced Yeats so it rhymed with beets.

By Monday, you couldn't swing a cat in Switchback without hearing another story about Rodney Hardwick. He had traveled around during the Depression with a troupe of players, setting up in vacant lots. Chautauqua, he called it. There was music and juggling, and Harlan. himself had been the dramatic reader. He did scenes from *Macbeth* and recited epic poems like *The Rime of the Ancient Mariner.* "Water, water all around and not a drop to drink." That one always brought the house down in the Dust Bowl, he said. He and his wife moved to North Dakota where she taught English in the high school, and the two of them put on plays in barns and schoolhouses to help make ends meet. The wife died; he took off for California. Woody Guthrie slept on his floor for six months. He asked Rodney to be Arlo's godfather, but Rodney, not a church-going man, declined. He roomed with Richard Burton and they heated canned beef stew over a hot plate for dinner. He once did the balcony scene from *Romeo and Juliet* with Dame Edith Evans, for the troops in Guam, constructing the balcony out of a platform lashed to a palm tree.

Dinner parties were thrown in profusion that winter in Switchback, with Rodney the frequent guest of honor. He paid for the hospitality with a poem or a story, and no one complained when he slept over on their sofas rather than going back to his cot at the Landslide. He was a gentleman through and through. He addressed the women like they were royalty, the men like they were stout-hearted. He was generous with his stories, sharing them with children, the guys down at the bar and Switchback's most prominent citizens without discrimination. Rodney was better than the single fuzzy TV station they got out of Grand Junction. He was better than books.

Rodney's heart swelled with gratitude toward the good people of Switchback. "I would be honored," he announced after a particularly satisfying dinner, "if this fine village would allow me, its humble servant, to produce a small dramatic production for its enjoyment." That is how Rodney talked. You halfway expected him to make a low courtier's bow, sweeping the floor with a large, plumed hat.

"The title shall be 'Love's Light Wings,' a phrase borrowed from Romeo and Juliet," said Rodney in his interview for *The Tailings*. "Taking works by Shakespeare, the Immortal Bard, the players will perform scenes about that most sublime of human emotions," he continued. He promised them music, romance and verse, an event "the likes of which has not been seen in the high country since the appearance of Jenny Lind onstage at the Opera House in Leadville in 1851."

So much of Switchback was involved in the production that it was hard to imagine where the audience was going to come from. Frankie Contino constructed a stage in the school gym, framing it with some old curtains he found in the furnace room. His girlfriend, Madge, who had brown hair that fell to her waist, agreed to be Juliet in the balcony scene. She would play opposite Andrew Carlyle, a handsome blond Aspen ski patroller who once got his picture in National Geographic doing a backward flip over a St. Bernard dog. Harlan wrote a newspaper story, and Betty and Pat at the Chamber of Commerce mimeographed it and mailed it out all over Colorado.

"Love's Light Wings" went forward. There were no auditions; Rodney just cast everyone as he saw fit, let them be themselves, and that was that. He announced who got the parts before the tryouts; in fact, there *were* no tryouts.

He invited Darlene to read "How Do I Love Thee?" and she accepted with delight. He complimented Nick's booming baritone and asked if he would sing an Elizabethan ballad. Then he told everyone in Switchback they would be there on the third Saturday in January, and they were.

Suits and ties came out of closets. Wrinkles were pressed out of cocktail dresses. "Just wear your hiking boots to the door of the school, and then slip on your high heels once you're inside," advised Ella. "Like we always do."

Andrew, a reckless Romeo, showed up drunk or scared--no one knew which--and forgot his lines immediately. He tried to ad-lib in his own version Olde English, no easy task for someone whose sole stock of adjectives consisted of "groovy" and "bummer." He hung his head before a shocked Juliet and murmured, "Oh, alas and alack. Alas and alack." Sensing a need to pick up the tempo, Madge gave her "wherefore art thou" speech without further ado and Romeo, clutching his silken cap, staggered into the wings. The applause was practically deafening.

During Nick's Romantic Ballad Number, someone let his German shepherd in because she was barking outside in the cold. Sniffing the smell of greasepaint, she found her way to her master and curled herself at his feet, but not before emitting a fart that, although not loud, was detected as far as the back rows. Nick got a polite hand at the end, but it was the dog whose picture appeared in the Thursday paper above the caption, "Fair is foul and foul is fair."

In spite of it all, "Love's Light Wings" was an unqualified success, the most entertaining event to come to Switchback since the Oddfellows brought the World's Best Whistler up from Pueblo. The following Monday, still surfing the wave of public enthusiasm, Harlan and Darlene convened a meeting at The Chamber of Commerce, inviting all of Switchback's business owners.

"We stand at the threshold of a new era," boomed Harlan. "We're sitting on a gold mine here."

"Rodney is a national treasure," Darlene said adoringly.

And so the S.A.C. was formed, the Switchback Arts Community. Dean Blevins, the real estate broker who was instrumental in developing the Echo Mountain Shoppette, would find them some land to buy. He thought the ghost town of Radio could be had for a song. They could fix up the old houses and form an institute of the arts. People would come from all over to study and perform. Rodney Hardwick himself would star in their first performance. Rodney, Harlan said, had recently confided to him about the enormous circus tent his old troupe transported from town to town, how they played to full houses all across Nebraska and Iowa. With the proceeds from the upcoming benefit, Harlan said with conviction, they could buy their *own* theater tent. People would be driving up to Switchback from Denver, not the other way around, to see the best plays in the West. It was a sure thing. The first step would be to throw a dinner to raise some funds.

Fifteen dollars a plate wasn't cheap in those days. Minimum wage was still below three dollars an hour; that's what Madge made in the real estate office on weekends, typing contracts and answering the phone. But the turn-out at the benefit dinner was huge. Citizens chewed happily on their dinners and complimented the wine. Artichokes, a puzzling new vegetable from California, cost extra, but nearly everyone ordered one when they learned the full proceeds from their sale would be donated to the theatre tent project. Harlan gave a speech, but it was Rodney who brought them to their feet with Robert Service's "The Cremation of Sam McGee," a poem in which an Alaskan prospector burns himself up in the fireplace in an effort to get warm. It's the kind of poem that people in high mountain towns can relate to, especially toward the end of January.

After paying the food bill, the S.A.C. netted slightly more than five hundred dollars. "A formidable sum," declared Rodney. "A good omen. We shall indeed have Macbeth in the summer."

Macbeth.

It gave them chills to think about it.

The rehearsals took place at Sonmeier's barn. It hadn't burned down yet; that was later on. They didn't dare meet inside the building, at least not until the skunks had their litters and moved on. No, Rodney and his company rehearsed outside, on the large platform where the hay was stacked before it was loaded onto wagons. It made a decent temporary stage, at least until the wonderful tent arrived. If they practiced in the morning, they could be pretty sure they wouldn't get rained on. The showers didn't start till after two in the afternoon; they came like clockwork all season long, except for when it hailed.

Of course, Rodney would play the Thane himself. At The Landslide recently, he'd given them goose bumps with his "Is this a dagger?" speech, a hint of the spectacle to come. With his raggedy troupe of players, he ran through the swordplay scenes in what was formerly the corral. Children sat on the fence rails to watch, and after they went home, they'd play Macbeth in their back yards, not quite sure of the plot, but thrilled with all the blood and dying.

Everyone in town was behind the project. No one dared to say it was too hoity toity--not in public at least--although the mayor thought next time they might try a melodrama with a villain. "Something in regular English," he said.

"We must aspire to be more than what we are," declared Mrs. Poole, and perhaps she was right.

Rodney, after tea with the ancient Vigil sisters one afternoon, announced that they had graciously accepted the parts of the three witches. Beulah Vigil, seventy years old, her wild hair the color of robins' eggs, was witch number one. Gladys, round as a barrel with a nose like a pig, nostrils pointing straight at you, was number two. Lois came along reluctantly as the final witch. She was the odd one. She insisted on wearing her baseball cap during rehearsals. She said she couldn't remember her lines unless her head was covered. Rodney, used to the temperament of artists, let her have her way. You can't do Macbeth with just two witches; it looks cheap.

There was a sultry redhead named Yancy, a drama major from Denver University who came to Switchback to student teach third grade, and she was cast, perfectly, as Lady Macbeth. Yancy's voice could shatter glass.

The sparkling white tent arrived two days before the performance. Harlan and Dean Blevins magnanimously signed the promissory note for the tent money while a reporter from *The Tailings* snapped their picture. The take from the first night's show would more than cover the nut this first month, they said with confidence. There was hand-shaking all round, and then the crew hit the road, declining a chance to purchase advance tickets at a reduced rate. "Looks like rain," said old man Sonmeier. He pulled his cap down tightly over his forehead.

"All is in readiness, my noble sir," said Darlene to Rodney at the final dress rehearsal, executing a near-perfect curtsy. Her recent habit of speaking in iambic pentameter had begun to get on people's nerves, but no one complained publicly. She and Harlan had done so much for the town.

The big day dawned dark and cloudy, but no amount of threatening weather could destroy the excitement felt in Switchback. It was said that all through Switchback you could hear happily whistled tunes, "There's No Business like Show Business," and "Another Openin', Another Show." Spirits were high, from the Chamber to the Coop. Everyone had a job to do, from setting up the benches to numbering the ticket stubs, to practicing his or her lines. So it wasn't until early afternoon that they all realized...Rodney was gone.

"Did you check the Landslide? Did you go to Sonmeier's?" Darlene asked worriedly. "I'm sure he's around here someplace."

"I think I saw his pickup headed over towards Leadville at six o'clock this morning," said Frankie. "It's a red Chevy, right?"

"Let's split up," suggested Harlan, ever the organizer. "Check every house. Check the river. We'll meet back here at three o'clock."

Switchback is not a large town. There is no place to hide out. There is no place to stash a car, nowhere to sit and drink a cup of coffee without running into half a dozen people you know. Someone called the police. Maybe he'd been in an accident. But no. Macbeth had simply vanished. The Thane had skipped, taking his truck and tools with him.

It was too late to cancel. The story had already come out in the Denver Post Weekend Edition. "Mountain Town Welcomes the Bard." People were already on the road, driving up for the show. Word was afoot that a Hollywood talent scout might be in the audience. John Denver was rumored to be driving over from Aspen. Mrs. Poole had promised her students extra credit if they showed up. The Landslide was putting on an after-the-show dinner, had purchased a whole case of avocados out of Denver for the guacamole.

No one was surprised by the rain, but the wind was the worst they had seen in years. Neighbors called neighbors on the phone. "Are you bringing a sleeping bag?" they asked. "I am. I'm not going to sit there freezing."

"What are you doing for footwear? I can't decide between hiking boots and galoshes."

Nick went into seclusion to practice his lines. He had been to every rehearsal and was Rodney's self-appointed understudy. Nick would pinch hit for Macbeth.

No one considered staying home. No one asked for his money back. In fact, the citizens of Switchback had the suspicion that Rodney Hardwick was playing some kind of good-natured tomfoolery on them. Maybe this was part of the show. They fully expected Rodney to descend from the sky onto center stage, suspended by a Peter Pan-style harness like some Elizabethan angel. They didn't know if it was in the plot, but they wanted it to be. He was such a showman, that Rodney.

The good news was that by show time, the rain had stopped. Patrons standing in line at the entrance to the tent swept the snow off each other's shoulders and stamped their feet. What was it that the old timers said? Ten months of winter and two months of tough sledding? They looked up at the sky and decided the old timers were right.

Later, everyone said it was the best that Macbeth could possibly be, unless you did it with real English accents, like Rodney's old pal, Richard Burton. They said this not only to be polite, which they were, but because it was true. The first gust of wind, the one that whipped the corner of the tent out of its stakes at stage right, blew just hard enough to reveal Beaulah's striped longjohns. By the time Lady Macbeth gave her "Out damned spot" speech, she had to yell to be heard above the crack of the thunder, but Yancy had a voice like a fog horn. Projection was her special gift, a useful thing for an elementary school teacher.

Nick botched his lines, but no one except Mrs. Poole knew the difference, and she watched her students, beaming, knowing that this, their first experience of theater, would remain with them forever. There would never be another Macbeth for them like this one. No banshee could utter a wail any eerier than the screaming tempest that circled the tent that night. Mrs. Poole's girl students clutched each other in terror; the boys, acting brave, watched the performance in silence, their eyes wide. It was better than any movie.

After a long standing ovation, with the muted clapping of mittened hands, the entire group, cast and audience, stomped through the wet snow to the Landslide. Jim, the bartender, invented a hot drink called the Rodney Toddy, mostly rum and sugar water, and they toasted their missing friend. "Must've got stage fright," said Jim. "He'll be back when he gets over it."

But he never was. Rodney never returned.

The only problem that remained was the twenty-five hundred dollars still owed on the tent. The Garden Club treasurer, experienced in fund-raising, suggested that Harlan and Dean purchase chrysanthemums to sell in order to pay off the note the two of them had so enthusiastically signed. For a year after that, any family in Switchback who was caught without a chrysanthemum on its kitchen table was considered downright unpatriotic. Old Mrs. Buchanan, the wealthy dowager who lived in the Forde mansion, finally bought out the lot of them and gave them to St. Theresa's for midnight mass, just to put the affair to bed once and for all.

When Sonmeier's barn burned to the ground, almost everyone forgot Rodney. They had no reference point anymore, no spot to point at and say, "This was the site of our greatest moment." It's a good argument for preserving the old buildings. We need something to look at, to remind us to tell the story. All that remains in Switchback now, thirty-some years later, is an abundance of hardy chrysanthemums growing along the alleys, thrown out some long-ago spring, too far back to remember.

WATERMELON SNOW

You hear the fall cattle drive before you see it. A mile up towards Ruby, the far-off sound of a restless herd can wake you up out of a sound sleep. There's the whistle of a cowboy keeping the animals together, the occasional shout. At first, you might think you're hearing motorcycle engines or chain-saws running; the low drone is exactly the same. But eventually, you realize it's cows, a herd coming down from the high pastures to the fields closer in, where they will live and feed until they're bred, or sold, or shipped off.

This may be the one-hundred-twentieth year that cattle have been driven up Main Street, past the Valley Forge restaurant, past the office of *The Tailings* newspaper office, past the thrift store of the Sunshine Girls, who have seen countless cattle drives by now. Still, everyone goes outside to watch. Maybe this is the year that Bert Spivak's grandson will ride his own horse behind the herd instead of sharing a saddle with his Mom, who grew up riding this same route in a time when the street was not yet paved. Maybe a frisky calf will dart down a side street or a trim cowboy will touch his finger to the brim of his hat as his eyes meet those of a girl watching from her window where she waters a red geranium plant.

Something about the cattle drive filled Katie with energy that morning. Like everyone else in town, she'd been awakened early, and the clean morning air had been invigorating. As the last of the herd crossed the highway and started down Evelyn Store Road for the final leg of its journey, Katie slid down off the fence rail she'd been watching from and walked the short distance back home. Her to-do list, scribbled on the back of a store receipt the night before, sat propped up on the kitchen table. *Fix TV.* That was easy. It just had a frayed cord. It appeared that a puppy had chewed it through. Katie hoped the set was disconnected when the act took place. It might have had disastrous results, like the time her cat, Trixie, urinated into the toaster, an act of rebellion that, although not fatal, caused her from that day forward to hide in the closet the moment Katie opened a package of bread. Katie wondered how many household accidents were caused by electric appliances. It is the kind of paranoia that makes her mother unplug everything before she leaves the house, even the clocks. Katie has instructed her sister that if she ever starts acting like that, Jill has permission to pour cold water over her head to snap her out of it. Hopefully, they will not be near any electrical appliances at the time.

Katie looked at the boxes stacked against her shed. At the garage sales where she'd purchased all this stuff, it had looked promising. The half-full cans of spray paint, the fake flowers, the box of ribbons saved from a long ago bridal shower. "This place looks like a pigpen hit it," she could hear her grandmother say. Seventy years in America and she never quite grasped the idioms. To her list, Katie scribbled: *clean up junk.*

She wound electricians' tape around the television's cord and plugged it in. Nothing. Determined to complete at least one item on her list today, she took a Phillips screw-driver and removed the back of the set. The innards clattered to the table in a jumbled heap. Katie stared at the hopeless mess of plastic and wire and then swept it into the trash. Bored, she reached for a can of paint and sprayed the outside of the cabinet red. Hm. Finding a partially-empty can of a color called Cumulus, she decorated the inside with blue swirls reminiscent of fluffy clouds.

But not until Katie saw the empty Chianti bottle in the recycle bin did her idea begin to take shape. Something about the bulbous vessel reminded her of her grand-mother's ample hips. She balanced an apple on the neck of the bottle. Skillfully, she cut a frock out of a remnant of cotton fabric. Then, turning her attention back to the television cabinet, she got out her hot glue gun and affixed dozens of colorful buttons to the top and sides. The apricot-colored rhinestones made her think of tea sugar, and tea sugar made her want to cry.

Her grandmother had so few possessions that it was possible to memorize them, a game Katie created for herself in the hours she was left to her own devices while the old woman scrubbed her floors or worked in the garden. This is not a bad thing for a child. A child doesn't have to be playing soccer or taking piano lessons every moment of the day to keep from being bored, Grandma knew. So when her grandmother was busy, Katie sometimes walked around her flat, looking at her things.

The tea sugar was mysterious to her. They didn't have anything like it at home. It didn't look like sugar at all, but like peach-colored crystals of rock candy.

"What is this stuff?" she asked, pointing to the slim glass jar on the pantry shelf when she was five or six years old.

"You can read. Tea sugar," her grandmother said.

"Where did you get it?"

Grandma wiped her hands on the apron she always wore. "In my first job in this country I was a chambermaid at a big hotel downtown. That was before I ever met your grandfather. One of the guests was a beautiful lady from Vienna. She used to talk to me. She asked me where I was from. My home town was not so far from Vienna, about half a day on the train. I was homesick and she let me talk. One day she gave me a cup of tea with this sugar in it. I was so afraid I would get into trouble with the boss for drinking tea with a rich lady! When she checked out, she told me to keep this jar of sugar, as a present."

"Do you ever use it?" Katie had asked.

"Oh, no. It's much too nice."

"It's pretty," said Katie. "It's golden, like honey."

Late in the afternoon, Ron Martinez appeared at Katie's gate with a bunch of lettuce in his hand. "I had to pick it before it bolted," he explained. "Did you hear me on the radio?" he asked. "I interviewed the potato weevil guy." Ron had a weekly gardening show called *All The Dirt*.

"I forgot," said Katie. "I guess I got busy." She waved a glue gun in the air as if to illustrate the point.

"No problem," said Ron. "The earthworm show was better. What's that?" he said, pointing at the former television set, its surface bejeweled with a mosaic of colorful plastic buttons.

"It's my grandmother," said Katie. She watched as he peered through the plastic screen at the pear-shaped figure of an old-country peasant, a fringed babushka over her carved-apple head.

"My grandmother looked like that too," said Ron. "Only she wore an apron."

"Apron. Good idea," said Katie. She took a piece of calico and cut a square, fastening it around the Chianti bottle with a blue ribbon. "Apron it is. You can't make potica without an apron."

"Potica?" he asked.

"It's a long story. Some other time," she said.

"It reminds me of those graves up on Potato Hill," said Ron. "The ones with all the plastic flowers and collections of stuff? The ones that look like little shrines?"

Katie nodded. "And now Doris Trujillo is gone, too, buried up there with all the others. I didn't see you at the wake last week."

"I was there early," said Ron. "I helped move the tables into the activity room before I went to work."

"Well, those plastic flowers were amazing. Every color of pink you can imagine. It was all everybody talked about. That and her outfit. Fuschia-colored velour."

"Tell me more about your grandmother," Ron said.

"Grandma would have liked it in Switchback. She came from a little mountain village in Slovenia. After grandpa died, all she did was paint. She was an artist, but it took her sixty years to get started."

"Looks like you inherited the gift," Ron said.

"I'm no artist. I'm just a glue-er. It's missing something, though," said Katie, crossing her arms and squinting at the television with a critical eye. "Some natural objects. Grandma loved nature."

"There's not much room left in there. You could take the harmonica out," suggested Ron.

"The harmonica stays. She played Strauss waltzes on one just like it."

"And the paint brushes?"

"They're essential. We'll just rearrange them a bit. That'll make room for some pine cones and feathers."

"OK," said Ron. "Let's go shopping."

Soon they were bumping along in Ron's pickup truck. "The sign says this road is closed," Katie warned. "Are you sure you know where you're going?"

"That's just for the tourists," Ron said confidently. He gunned the engine to ease the tires over a slippery rise.

"How old is this truck, anyway?"

"Got it in 1982." said Ron, patting the dash. "Two hundred fifty-one thousand miles."

"Wow," Katie said. "My car is only twelve years old."

"Take good care of it," Ron advised. "You'll get another twelve out of it."

"I hope so. I like used things. Stuff, clothes, even cars."

"Me, too," Ron said.

"My grandma would've liked you. She lived more simply than anyone I've ever known."

"Cool."

"You want to hear a story? You see, even though she lived in America most of her life, Grandma always spoke with a heavy accent. She got her words mixed up all the time. So one day the neighbor lady called Grandma over to see their new car. It was really fancy. Push-button windows, air conditioning, the works. The payments were huge, they bragged. Well, Grandma thought it was a crime, a real waste of money. She shook her head and said, 'Enough is too much.'

"Don't you mean enough is enough, Grandma?" I asked her. "That's how they say it in English."

'You say it your way, I'll say it mine,' she said."

"Enough is too much," said Ron with admiration. "Makes sense to me."

Ron stopped the truck where a rocky snowslide blocked their path. He shifted into first, pulled out the emergency brake, and cut the engine. For a moment the two of them sat silently, looking through the windshield at the brilliant, treeless landscape. An ancient bristlecone pine, its branches twisted close to the ground, cast a sharp shadow.

The ruffled leaves of low-growing saxifrage peeked out from between dark rocks. Lichen grew in every color, from lime green to orange to gray, its feathered edges spreading out in overlapping circles.

Their first time up at this elevation, backyard gardeners might attempt to kidnap a few plants and take them home. They imagine them growing in rock gardens near their patios, with stalwart high-altitude stonecrop coexisting next to their domestic geraniums. But although these mountain plants are among the hardiest in the world, they do not take to civilization. They will not be transplanted to warmer, friendlier climes. They will not be messed with, and if you move them, or water them, or try to make them a home in your own backyard garden, they will die on you.

"I haven't been up on the tundra for years," said Katie. "Early fall like this is the best time. I'd forgotten how clear it is up here, like looking through a lens."

"There's a brown-capped rosy finch," Ron said, pointing to a bird flying low over pillow of spongy moss. "The bugs must be hatching out of the snow."

"Insects live in snow?" Katie asked, surprised.

Ron nodded. "Let's go up there," he said, pointing at a gentle hill. "The snow's pretty deep. We'll have to post-hole."

The drifts came up to their hips. "Ick. Looks like something died here," said Katie, pointing to a huge red stain on the surface of the snow.

"It's watermelon snow," Ron said. "Last of the season. Have some. Not too much, though. It'll give you the runs."

"Oh, yeah, have something that will give me the runs. Are you crazy?"

Ron scooped out a small handful and licked at it. "Even tastes like watermelon." He held it out to her.

Gingerly, Katie took a lick. "It does," she said. "What's the deal?"

"It's algae. It lives deep down in the snow banks. Then, as the days get longer, it swims to the surface and turns red. The red color seems to protect it from harmful ultraviolet rays. Eventually, the insects and other microorganisms eat it. Basically, it's at the bottom of the food chain up here."

"Sometimes I feel like *we're* on the bottom of the food chain," Katie said. "Especially you. You don't eat meat. You grow all your own food."

"You don't even buy retail," Ron said. "Everything you own was used by someone else first."

"We're at the bottom and the rich are at the top," Katie said. "It takes all of us to support them. Maids, carpenters, cooks, landscapers."

"Could be worse," Ron said. "The bottom is closer to the earth. Still, you'd think they'd realize how much damage they do. They drive those big new cars and knock down perfectly good houses to build bigger ones, and then they only stay in them a couple of weeks a year. And they seem proud of it all. Someone should tell them to stop."

"It's like Grandma used to say," said Katie. "You can drive a horse to drink but you can't make him water."

"You can say that again," said Ron, offering Katie his hand as she stepped over a fallen log on the way back to the truck.

SWEAT SUIT

In love I pay my endless debt to thee for what thou art.

Rabindranath Tagore
from the journal of Norman Sanger

They buried Doris Trujillo on Potato Hill, dressed in hot pink velour, a long string of pearls around her neck. It was her best outfit. Cleaned and steam pressed, it had hung in a plastic dry cleaning bag at the back of her closet since New Year's Eve. It looked warm and soft, comfortable enough to sleep in.   Other   women *would* have slept in it. After all, it was a sweat suit. Old ladies in Switchback call them lounging suits. Or, as Doris referred to it often, "That beautiful outfit my husband gave me for our anniversary when he was in the hospital."

Doris passed on a week after her 78th birthday, on a night that smelled of Indian corn and apple cider. Her grandson, Kyle, dreamed that night of skateboarding through a rainbow of crystals, never touching down, watching the earth from treetop level. Her daughter, Maria, also asleep, felt a chill and pressed her body against the warm back of her husband, Andy. He rolled over and buried his face in her shoulder, the softness of her hair sending him sweetly into a dream.

Doris herself dreamed of being borne gently upwards on the smoke of campfires till she reached the edge of a white cloud and was pulled aboard by Lou, her husband, gone for a long time now. Feeling young and bold and curious, Doris leaned over the edge of the cloud and saw the people of the Switchback, like dots of light, sleeping in their beds. She saw her old friend, Ida, glowing soft and blue like the moon. Maria, her firstborn, a golden spark. She saw her own light, like the memory of a firefly's path, spiral up to the cloud where Lou now held her hand. Lights everywhere, like a holiday. It reminded her of the night Lou proposed to her long ago, under a string of clear bulbs in the old pavilion in Wilson Park.

The week of their forty-ninth anniversary, just eight short years ago, Lou lay in his hospital bed in Grand Junction, watching rain splash into puddles in the parking lot. He was the color of woodstove ashes. Next to him on a hard chair sat his wife, Doris, her wrinkled hand covering his own. Her nails, always beautiful, were painted Fuchsia Fantasy; it was her favorite color. The two girls, Maria and Pilar, stood on either side of the bed.

"It's going to be all right, Ma," Maria said. "The surgeon said they got the tumor out."

"He's never been sick before," said their mother.

"He'll get better now," Pilar reassured her. "He'll just need a lot of rest. The doctor says he can come home in a week."

"A week! That's after our anniversary," said Doris. She turned to her husband. "We'll wait and celebrate when you come home," she said.

"Okay," Lou said. He looked down at his shrunken body and over at the hospital meal that had just been delivered to his room. Chicken broth and vanilla pudding. "I don't care how much weight I'm losing on this diet," said Lou, a big man all his life. "I want some real food. Green bean casserole."

"You hate green bean casserole," Pilar said.

Doris smiled. "It's good to hear you make a joke," she said, poking him teasingly in his skinny arm. "You must be getting well." She smiled bravely. "Let's have a nice forty-ninth anniversary party right here in your room. I'll get some of those shiny balloons. We'll make up some enchiladas. No pork. The nurses say you have to watch your diet. I'll go out and invite them to come to the party right now."

When Doris was gone, Lou motioned for Pilar and Maria to come closer. "I didn't get your mother anything for our anniversary," he whispered. "I've never missed a year."

"You couldn't," said Maria. "You've been sick. She'll understand."

"Buy her something, okay? Put my name on it. I'll give you the money when I get out of here."

"All right," said Maria. "What do you think she'd like?"

"You figure it out. I'm sick. Remember."

"You'll do anything to get out of shopping," Pilar said.

"Just get her something nice," Lou said. "And pick up a card, too. Something romantic."

"We'll have to be sneaky," said Maria. "We're together twenty-four hours a day lately. By the time we leave the hospital and drive home at night, everything's closed. The only shopping you can do around here is in that gift shop downstairs where they sell the newspapers."

"Do your best," Lou said. "And it better be nice. She's a saint, your mother."

"Time for his nap," a cheerful nurse announced, returning to the room with Doris. "Why don't you ladies go down to the cafeteria and have a cup of tea?"

"We could go shopping," suggested Pilar brightly.

"It's pouring out there," said Doris. "Let's just go to that little store downstairs. I want to buy your father something to read."

In the gift shop, Doris paid for a newspaper and glanced over at a mannequin wearing a fuchsia sweat suit. "That's a nice outfit," she said to the girls. "My favorite color." She walked over and squinted at the price tag. The girls heard her snort. "I don't care how pretty it is," she said disgustedly.

"What do you mean?" asked Pilar.

"It may be nice, but it's not worth three hundred sixty dollars," said Doris.

"Ouch," Pilar said. "What a rip off."

It was later that day that Maria excused herself, saying she needed to get some fresh air. She checked the price tag on the sweat suit in the gift shop and laid it on the counter by the register. "You're not going to believe this," she laughed as she handed two twenty dollar bills to the clerk. "But my mom thought the price tag said three hundred sixty dollars. Not thirty-six."

"This is Grand Junction," said the clerk. "Not Aspen. She must have read the zeros wrong. Maybe she needs glasses. Would you like that gift wrapped?"

No bunch of shiny balloons and Happy Anniversary banners can make a hospital room seem like home, but Doris was so glad to know that Lou was getting well that her cheer was contagious. She poured champagne into paper cups and passed it around, winking at the nurses when she told them it was Seven-Up. She led the singing of Cielito Lindo, the first song that she and Lou had ever danced to. The girls presented their parents with matching scarves to wear when the winter came.

"One-hundred percent wool!" Doris exclaimed. "So extravagant! Polyester would have been just fine. We'll just put this aside for a special occasion." Pilar rolled her eyes at Maria.

Maria shyly handed Lou a small wrapped package, a framed picture of the two of them on their wedding day.

At last, Lou handed his wife her present, which he'd hidden behind his pillow as soon as the girls had delivered it to him. "Happy anniversary, honey," he said. "I love you."

To Doris, With Love, from Lou. Doris removed the wrapping, all the while explaining how beautiful the ribbon was, how shiny the paper. Loving the anticipation, she slowly lifted the lid and tore the gold paper seal that held the tissue paper together. "Oh my God," she whispered when she saw the rich fuscia fabric underneath.

It was the suit. Plush hot pink velour, as rich as sheared mink. Tears came to her eyes.

"Oh, Lou. My God. Take it back. It's too good for me."

"It's not exactly a fur coat," Lou said.

"This is the most beautiful thing you've ever given me," Doris cried. "I just can't believe it."

"It's just a lounging suit, Doris," he said. "But the color is nice. It matches your nails," he added practically.

"It's gorgeous," she said. "I'll only wear it for very, very special occasions. When you get out of here, we'll have a nice, candlelight dinner at home, just the family, and I'll wear this." She said it reverently, like another woman might breathlessly describe a perfect diamond.

Doris stroked the velour with a trembling hand. "I have to show the nurses. I won't tell them how valuable it is," she added. "It might make them feel bad. On their salaries." She gathered up the box and left the room, leaving Lou with the daughters.

"What's going on?" he asked. "Doesn't she think I can afford a thirty-six dollar sweat suit?"

"She thinks it cost three hundred sixty dollars," said Pilar, laughing. "She checked the price tag in the gift shop but she didn't have her glasses on."

Lou shook his head. "Oh, boy," he said. "Your mother."

Maybe it was the close brush with death, having surgery and all. But Lou started to feel guilty. He was basically an honest man. So when he got out of the hospital, he called Maria. "You have to tell your mother the truth about that sweat suit," he said.

"I'm not going to tell her; *you* tell her," Maria said.

"*I* can't tell her. She thinks I'm some kind of sugar daddy now. I'd seem like a cheapskate."

"You want *me* to tell her you're a cheapskate then?" said Maria.

"Come on," he said, but that was the end of it.

Lou died some years later, suddenly, of a heart attack. It was a long time before Doris wanted to go visiting, but she finally did, to a Christmas party hosted by the Wozniaks across the street.

"I wore that beautiful outfit your father gave me," she told Maria the next day. "I was the best-dressed woman there. Oscar Rohde gave me the eye. I already took it to the dry cleaner," she went on. "I want it to last."

"And now it's lasted long enough," said Maria to Pilar as they looked down at their mother's peaceful face.

Lost in their thoughts, they didn't hear when Jane Wozniak came up behind them.

"Her favorite outfit," Jane said .

"She was so proud of it," said Pilar.

"She was. Even after she found out it only cost thirty-six dollars," said Jane.

Pilar and Maria looked at her with a start, their eyes widening.

"She found the price tag on the waistband the first time she wore it," said Jane. "She told me the whole story. Made me promise never to say a word. But I think it's all right to tell you now, don't you?"

"Did she ever tell Dad?" Pilar asked.

"Lord, no. She thought he'd make her go out and get her eyes checked. She said glasses would make her look like an old lady."

She always was proud of her looks, agreed Maria. "Just look at that manicure."

Pilar smiled. "It was always her favorite color."

GOING HOME

Katie drove over to Goldflake on Saturday, anxious to make one last trip over Independence Pass before it closed for the season. It could happen any day now. Once a storm hit, the highway department stopped plowing the road, snapping padlocks on the gates on both sides to keep drivers from attempting the icy, steep climb. From the top of the pass, Katie noticed some dark, wet clouds closing in. There would probably be a dusting of snow on the high peaks by morning.

Katie's old friend, Martha, was opening a bookstore-cafe. Onomotopizza, read the invitation. Poetry, Pizza, Pizzazz!

"You have to get their attention," said Martha, pointing up at the well-lit sign. "Competition is keen these days, with all the chain restaurants moving in."

Dick Harris was there, sipping red wine from a plastic glass. "How are the kids?" Katie asked. She had been their favorite babysitter the year she arrived.

"Briggita's got a tattoo. Ben's hugging trees. Say, I hear you moved up to Switchback," he said. "I was there a few years back. It's like this place used to be."

"Not for long," said Katie. "They're talking about second golf course."

"Hell, we have four. At least you don't have twenty-one T-shirt shops.

"Goldflake has twenty-one T shirt shops?"

"Count 'em."

"I drove over for Martha's opening. Things sure are jumping around here, compared to the old days."

"Yeah. There's no more Bingo at the fire house. Now they call it Las Vegas Night and Leona makes me wear a sports jacket. The high school cafeteria has a sushi bar. Speaking of food, want to stop by for supper?"

"Sure. You still live behind the post office?"

"No one's called it that for years. It's a timeshare office now. Same place, though."

"See you around six, then," said Katie. "I'm going to take a walk up Goat Creek."

"You mean Angora Heights. They won't let you past the guard house. It's our newest gated community."

"Thanks for the warning. How about Marmot Lake? Is that steep footpath still there?"

"It's the same, at least till they figure out how to pave the trail and charge for the air you breathe. They're working on it, though."

A furry pika squeaked at Katie from a pile of rocks at the trailhead. Two ravens soared overhead, calmly catching the updrafts. The air shimmered, dusty with the pollen of evergreen trees. The sunlight was a palpable thing, something you could almost reach up and touch.

Katie came across the familiar ruin of an old miner's cabin, nothing but a few logs now. Once she'd found a lady's leather shoe here, with a high heel and a tiny metal buckle. She thought about the woman whose small foot had fit into it. They tell you that mountain life was brutal a hundred years ago, but Katie believes the woman's heart soared every spring when the pasque flowers bloomed outside her door, and thanked her lucky stars every time she drank from the crystal stream that ran through her back yard. Maybe things were hard sometime, but city life wasn't all that great then, either.

Katie, too, has left personal objects in this very place. An apple core, left on a rock for a marmot to carry off. The button from a denim jacket. Human beings are careless that way, leaving bits and pieces of their lives about. Katie still comes across friends and stories that she left here in Goldflake, like objects that fell out of her backpack on her way to another life.

You never can gather all your stuff in the same place again once you have lived in one spot for as long as Katie lived in Goldflake. Even the people who stayed only one season left their traces, a story about how they found their way home in a blizzard, or their face in the town photo on Burro Day, now hanging on the wall of the city hall basement.

Katie still thinks of Goldflake as her home. People know her here; that's the comfortable part. She doesn't have to explain her history to them; they already know it. These folks were here the day she came to town. They introduced themselves and found her a place to live, the room behind the gift shop, and that year for Christmas she baked potica for all the families she babysat for, because by then they were friends. They came to her wedding.

When you come back home, Katie thought, you don't have to explain things. No one here is shocked anymore to hear that Katie's husband died when Eric was so little. It's an old story to them now. They were around when it happened. They backed off and watched as she made her way again. They tell her to send their love to Eric the next time she writes him. He always was a good kid, they say. "He still is," she likes to reply. "He kept me going," she tells her closest friends. "Without Eric, I wouldn't have had a reason to get up in the morning." They nod, remembering. She thinks she ought to tell Ron about it. He probably thinks she's divorced, not widowed. People usually do.

She was a maid then, at the town's only hotel. The rooms had televisions but no phones. Guests had to walk down to Main Street to make a telephone call. Maybe they ran into some ski bum who invited them over to his place for spaghetti. Maybe they talked to some old geezer in a bar, who showed them a gold nugget he carried in his shirt pocket, and it became their story; it became what they remembered about this place. Things are different now. Now, people remember if the remote control didn't work and they had to call the front desk for a replacement. They remember that the sewer backed up and they couldn't flush the toilet all morning. That's what they tell you about their visit to these magnificent mountains. That's the way their stories go now.

Picking her way up the stream, Katie thought about the funeral of Doris Trujillo, which she attended last week on Potato Hill. The obituary didn't say much; if you didn't know her, you might not know what a special person she was. She certainly wasn't what you would call famous. When a person is famous, the newspaper writes a long obituary, but no one is famous in Switchback. Regular people have to rely on their friends to provide their epitaph, and all you can do to slant it in your favor is to be a good neighbor while you are alive. Be cheerful. Wave hello over the backyard fence. Learn people's names. Say them out loud. Mornin', Ida. How's it going, Ned?

THREE HUNDRED DOLLARS

"To be wealthy, a rich nature is necessary."
                                        Norman Sanger

Martha, her old friend, had been suitably impressed when Katie told her about the offer from *Western Trends* Magazine. "Say something about my restaurant!" she begged.

"It's supposed to be a story about Switchback. They want me to write about Potato Day."

"Oh, all right. But when they hire you to do a story about Goldflake, just remember to say I use all natural ingredients and imported Parmesan. I'm going to make enough money this year go to Europe next spring. Can you believe it? Me? Who used to live in a teepee up Desolation Gulch that I rented for fifteen bucks a month?"

Like Martha, Katie remembers what she paid for everything she has ever bought. Though some people might think this is a special gift, it is actually a curse. It makes people with whom you are conversing yawn and change the subject. Katie is old enough now to understand this. Let a middle-aged woman talk too much and people think she's batty. Katie does not want to be thought of as batty, at least not until she deserves it, and she doesn't deserve it yet.

Children, they can get away with jabbering. They'll tell you what they saw on the way to school, every dog and mud puddle. They will share with you the details of the dream they had last night and you might say, "How interesting!" But if you care about their futures, don't praise them too profusely; it might backfire. What is adorable in a four-year-old is not always attractive in a grown person.

Sometimes, working the cash register at Theodora's, Katie meets a man who is, as Aunt Faye might say, full of himself. It's his mother's fault, thinks Katie. She shouldn't have told him he was so cute when he was little. She shouldn't have let him talk so much, bragged about all those big grown-up words he used. She should have told him to put a cork in it. Then he wouldn't be standing here telling Katie why *Happy Days* was better than *Taxi*. He wouldn't be describing in detail the sound system he just upgraded to in his car, and Katie's eyes wouldn't be glazing over with the boredom that comes right before sleep. He would be home with his wife. But of course he doesn't have a wife. That's why he goes shopping, to have a captive audience, if only for a short time. In his own mind, he thinks of it as having a conversation, but Katie would not describe it thus.

So Katie never tells people she has this ability to remember prices, keeping it to herself. No one knows that her first Hula Hoop, a blue one, was $2.06. It was money she had saved, and the six cents was tax. Her Visible Man plastic model kit was $6.18. Gingham fabric, thirty-six inches wide, was ninety-eight cents a yard when she made her first apron in home ec, and the first time she ever bought her own lunch in a restaurant it came to just over two dollars, a price she stuck to, stubbornly, until her twenties. Only it didn't buy as much any more. Two dollars used to buy a hamburger deluxe, fries and coleslaw, plus a medium Coke. Later it was downsized to a grilled cheese plate at Woolworth's. Now, as everyone knows, that very same amount will get you a Coffee of the Day at The Valley Forge. Her first movie ticket cost thirty-five cents and she has paid as much as ten dollars, and they say if you go to New York it's even more. She once bought a valuable painting for twenty-five dollars at a rummage sale. She has never paid more than thirty dollars for a dress, not even one to get married in.

But the number Katie is stuck on is three hundred dollars. Not that she hasn't paid more for things. She owns a car and she has done some traveling, both big-ticket items. But three hundred dollars is still the figure against which Katie measures all value. It is a yardstick. It has been the recurring number in her family since before the First World War. For almost one hundred years, the milestones in the lives of Katie's people have carried a price tag, and the price was always the same. Three hundred dollars.

Katie's grandmother was sent at age fifteen to come to America. The second-oldest of ten children, she was singled out to be the one to leave. "There were too many mouths to feed," she told Katie. "So they sent me away." Tears still formed in her eyes sixty years later when she told the story.

"My Aunt Mary wrote my father a letter from Chicago, where she had a job as a cook in a big house. They needed another servant, and Mary sent for me. Even though I wasn't the oldest, I was the responsible one. Mary sent the money to cover my travel costs. I worked hard and paid her back in two years. Three hundred dollars. That's what it cost to get from Slovenia to Chicago, traveling steerage class. That would cover the train fares in both countries, the boat trip, and food along the way. My father put Mary's letter in his pocket, and the next day he went to the city and purchased my ticket. Of course, we didn't call them dollars over there, but that's what it amounted to. Three hundred dollars."

It was many years before she met Katie's grandfather, and after accepting his proposal, she went back to her room and counted the bills under her mattress. The day of her wedding, she showed up at his sisters' house with a dress she had borrowed, and when he came into the kitchen for a beer before the ceremony, there not being any rules in those days about seeing the bride before the ceremony, she handed him three hundred dollars. All her savings.

The famous Oscar Meyer was the caterer for their wedding, she told Katie. Only he was not well known then, just another Old Country chef. The dinner was sausages and potatoes, potica, wine, and every immigrant in the whole neighborhood showed up. The bill, Grandma told Katie, was three hundred dollars. "Easy come, easy go," Katie's grandpa had said.

When Katie was little, her family was the first on Beech Avenue to have a television set. What did it cost? Three hundred dollars, her dad told her when she asked. In a book she read recently about the nineteen-fifties, Katie was interested to see that the average annual salary in those days was three *thousand* dollars. Imagine paying so much for a TV, one-tenth of what you made in a year.

Katie decided to leave college and go West. Her roommate, Polly, and Polly's boyfriend, Zig, drove her to her old neighborhood to withdraw the savings from her account at The First Bank. She had deposited the first few dollars into that account after her tenth birthday. The teller compared her eighteen-year-old signature to her childhood scrawl and asked to see her drivers' license to make sure she was the same person. The balance was three hundred dollars. Katie put it in her purse and said thank you. Polly wondered if the bank teller would think she needed the money for an abortion, because three hundred dollars was what they cost in those days, when they were illegal. One of the girls at college had one and everyone found out. She got deathly sick afterward. They had to take her to the hospital. She had this terrible infection. Her name was Laura and she had the most beautiful auburn hair and she dated Zig's roommate, David. David was incredibly smart. He was going to be a lawyer someday. He was a Jew and Laura was a Catholic and they both made the honor roll every quarter. After her abortion she didn't come back to school. David married another classmate, the dumpy, loudmouthed Judy Something-or-other. It was the seventies by then, and David drove a cab while Judy worked in an insurance office. They had degrees. Katie did not, but she was hired by a community college to teach classes in typing for six dollars an hour, more than Judy and David were earning at the time. Of course, Katie thinks, now they are probably very successful and rich, while she, Katie, only has the job at Theodora's Consignments.

Katie spent the three hundred dollars traveling Highway One, hitchhiking up and down between L.A. and San Francisco, just for the heck of it. Four months later, almost broke, she was offered a ride to Colorado, where she got two jobs that allowed her to work an entire forty-hour week in three days, Friday through Sunday. She started out at High Mountain Housemaids at eight in the morning, ran across the street to the Red Rooster at five, and waited tables until closing. The last diner usually left by ten in the evening and she had her shift drink at the bar along with a piece of chicken, and then she went home to sleep. She worked three fourteen-hour days in a row every week, but she was young. Minimum wage was $2.65 per hour, and for waitressing even less, but of course there were tips. A dollar was a big tip at the Red Rooster. Often on week-nights she babysat for families in the small town at fifty cents per hour per child. Families would double up, and some nights she sang Puff the Magic Dragon to half a dozen toddlers before they fell asleep on the living room floor, slumber party style. She ate whatever the kids ate and had permission to do her laundry at her clients' homes. It became a game to her to see how little she could get by on. There were even marvelous bonuses, like the summer she got to go to Europe as a nanny for the McIntyre children, and she stayed on for a few extra months after the family returned to the U.S. for the school year.

Her second winter in Goldflake, Katie met the man she was to marry, and they took off for what ended up being a four-month road trip. The money she dumped out of the jar she kept beneath her bed on the day they took off? The same three hundred dollars. By now it was no surprise.

They eventually bought their first house, a tiny two-bedroom shanty perched on the edge of a mountain. It cost exactly what her parents had paid for their huge four-bedroom home in the suburbs, but that was in 1955. Katie adored that house and worked hard with her husband to make the payments. What did they amount to? Three hundred dollars and fourteen cents, the approximate cost of the headstone for her husband after he died in an avalanche nine years later.

For Katie, that will always be the significant number. She wonders what number other people use, or if they even think about such things. It doesn't sound like much, when she gets the estimate from the auto mechanic or reads the prices on the menu outside of the Wine Kitchen Restaurant down on Main Street in Switchback. Some people Katie knows have phone bills that are higher than that. Some people pay that much for a hotel room for one night, and if it is in Rome or New York, they think they got a good deal. "I'd rather go camping," Katie says.

Listening to her friends, Katie realizes there are certain things people need in order to feel secure. Her friend, Violet, needs her grandmother's tea set. She says it makes her feel grounded. Violet's neighbor, Sarah, has said for years that all she needed was five thousand dollars. That would allow her to buy a car and get out of town, her lifelong dream. She is still waiting tables at the Valley Forge, and each year the required amount goes up, allowing her to stay a little longer.

Once, Katie met a man at a party in Aspen who said that if he only had three million dollars in the bank, he'd feel like he could take some time off and relax.

Katie is grateful that her needs are not as extravagant as all that. Alone in Europe, she'd imagined herself living in an English village forever. She adored having her morning coffee in a courtyard cafe amidst fragrant pots of lavender. She was enamored with English breakfasts, where they served the toast in a silver holder, the slices standing on end like books on a shelf.

Last year Katie saw a similar toast coffee that she brews herself, and experiences all the elegance she could possibly want, plucking a perfect slice of toast from its sterling rack.

ARBORGLYPHS

I am bound to this spot evermore.

Norman Sanger

There is a grove of trees on an overlook near McBain Pass to the south of Switchback, Colorado. Don't expect to find it easily, to spot it from your car while you drive by at sixty or even forty miles per hour. You may be going slow enough to see a deer grazing at the side of the road or a marmot sunning itself on a rock. But you will never see these unusual trees from the seat of your SUV. You will first have to turn east and cross a rickety cattle guard, and then go another rocky mile or two, to a gate locked with a chain. You will let your vehicle idle while you try the combination lock, to which someone will have to have given you the code, something they will only do if they feel you can be trusted. It's not like there's a number you can call and ask for the combination from your cell phone. This is a private road, and that means you.

Okay, you're in. You are careful to lock the gate behind you. Another hour on the bumpy dirt road, and you pull off and stop. There are roads everywhere and they are not marked. Someone gave you instructions to turn left one-point-seven miles from the deserted mine, and you'd better be watching your odometer or you have to back up and start again. Finally, you slow to a stop. You cut the engine and make your way across a muddy stretch that is bordered with orange-leafed rose bushes, their blood-red berries plump and tasting of apples. It's autumn, and even with your eyes closed, even if you were blind, you would be able to feel the light that seems to come from within the yellow aspen leaves that are everywhere now. No wonder the legend said the roads were paved with gold. They are. They are still.

There is no real path from here. You scramble over fallen aspen trees and climb the gentle, spruce-covered rise. You drop down the other side, kicking like a child through yellow leaves, and the view when you get to the edge is so huge that you may not see the carvings at all; you are drinking in the whole canvas of western Colorado with your astonished eyes.

But look to your right, if you remember. The aspen trees are ancient there. There is so much writing on them, it looks like newspaper. Manuelito Vasquez, El Basco Joselito, Juan de Roncesvalles. Carved fifty years ago, the writing stands out in dark, pencil-thick welts, the names melding into nature's blemishes, the teeth marks of a deer or a worm trail that scars the bark in a jagged line.

The carvings are high, almost out of your reach. That is because the Basque cowboys and sheepherders who made their marks here did so from the saddles of their horses. Looking across the western slope, they let their ponies graze, they rolled a cigarette, maybe, and they thought of the Pyrenees, of home. Carefully, with a sharp pocket knife, they etched their names on the white bark of an aspen tree, in a line so thin it barely showed up at all, not darkening for several years, as the tree grew around it. They wrote in a kind of script, neither printing nor cursive, but a graceful blend of the two. They added a figure of an elk with antlers, a horse, or a round-bodied nude woman. They etched the date. 1948. 1946. *This is the way I passed.*

Everyone has seen groves of monogrammed aspen trees along mountain roads in this country. Lovers still carve their initials on them, inside hearts. Kids cut in their names with new Boy Scout pocket knives. A joker might inscribe "Daniel Boone" on a tree and think he is fooling someone, but the Basque aspens are not like these. They are cut with a kind, delicate hand, scarcely scoring the tender white bark. The artist knows he will have to be patient. The letters will barely emerge for several years, but when they do, they will turn vivid and black, like oriental calligraphy, and they will speak a piece of history that barely made a ripple, anywhere. The life span of these trees is a short one hundred years.

Katie parked her beat-up Toyota at the edge of the meadow. She lifted the back hatch and withdrew the light-weight metal stepladder, setting it noisily on the ground. She checked her pockets for pencil, paper and knife. She hooked her plastic water bottle on her belt with a carabiner, picked up the ladder, and began to walk.

The ladder was awkward, too big to manage easily. Katie dragged it up and over the rise. She lifted it clumsily over the fallen trees, stopping to watch a magpie overhead. A good omen. A stark black and white magpie flying against a backdrop of quaking golden aspen branches is one of the most comely sights of autumn. In her pocket Katie carried a drawing of just such a bird, with open wings and long tail, copied from a wildlife book. She was no artist. For the purpose at hand, this simple tracing would be adequate.

Katie arrived at the overlook and dropped the ladder to the ground. Sitting on a boulder, she took a swig of water. Her heart pounded in her ears. It must be two thousand feet higher here than Switchback, she thought. She stared down into the valley. The gray, sparkling line of the Ruby River glittered far below her. Katie could not see the towns of Ruby and Switchback; they were blocked by hills--but the top of Echo Mountain was visible, sticking up through a heavy, wet October cloud.

It's hard to know how long Katie sat there. Probably less than an hour. Enough time for the gray cloud to continue its journey east. The sun broke out and warmed her face and a breath of wind, like a sigh, ruffled the hair on her head. It was time to begin.

Katie read the names. Diego Murillo. Victorio Salazar. She traced with her finger the drawing of a coffee pot above the name of Juan Villalobos. Then she chose a young aspen tree, about six inches in diameter. It stood slightly apart from the other saplings, in a clearing not far from where she had sat. Yellow and red holly surrounded its base like it had been planted there. She unfolded the ladder and stood on the third rung, her left hand leaning against the unblemished white trunk to support herself.

Opening her knife, Katie made a smooth, delicate, experimental cut. It was all but invisible. In lines as thin as a hair, she carved:

Katie

of

Switchback

Forever

She would make a map of this spot and leave it with a few friends. Maybe their children. Maybe next year, she would have a picnic here, bring them all out, drink chokecherry wine, and she'd point out the place she made her own mark.

Katie took the sheet of paper out of her pocket and held it against the tree as she carved through it, following the lines. Anyone, she thought, would recognize it as a magpie. She scored the wings with hatch-marks that would darken to black as the tree matured. It was a young aspen there was lots of time.

Katie inspected her work, putting a last touch on the magpie's eye. She sniffed the thin air and hoped the snow would wait until she got back on the paved road that led back to town.

FISH STORY

There is a phenomenon of light that occurs only at high elevations in the fall, and only when there is plenty of dust in the air. It happens when the sun is so low that it illuminates the bare tree limbs from the underside for a few short minutes before it sets. Everything looks so distinct, you might think you're having a metaphysical experience or something. But don't get excited. It's just the color and angle of the light. It's like the light some people see just before they get a migraine headache, but there's no pain. Pinpoints of luminescence swim in your field of vision, yellow and diffuse and filled with invisible twinkles of something like lightning bugs.

Maybe that's why so many fly fishermen go out on late fall afternoons. They are lured, as Ulysses was lured by the bewitching Sirens. Some guys, on the other hand, set out to hit golf balls at that golden hour. The new course is public; you can play on it for a fee. Depends on the kind of guy you are.

Ron is not a golfer. He is not a fly fisherman either, not any more, not since he quit eating meat ten years ago. But there was something about this particular light today. It almost sang. Its brightness was practically audible. Ron's wrist twitched, holding an imaginary rod. It felt pretty good, all things considered. Catch and release. What could be the harm?

It was the driest fall in years. Not since the thirties had it been this bad. Reporters from *The Tailings* were scrambling to find old-timers to reminisce about those days. "You could walk across the Ruby in your going-to-church shoes and never even get them wet," said Oscar Rohde in last Thursday's edition. "All the ditches dried up by August."

"There was so much dust we stuffed wet rags under the kitchen door to keep it from drifting into the kitchen," Ida concurred. "Even then, the biscuits had grit in 'em."

It was as just as arid this year, Ron observed as he stepped out of his pickup. The Ruby was dry from bank to bank, with only a thin trickle running down the center. Sometimes, the trickle went underground, leaving a bone-dry rock bed for a quarter mile at a stretch.

Upriver, Ron spotted a small puddle, dark as coal. Not much larger than a child's inflatable wading pool, it looked deep. Maybe a sinkhole, real old. Ron approached it, walking in the shadow of a cottonwood stand.

A two-foot silver shape trembled beneath the surface of the pool. "Damn, that's the biggest cutthroat I've ever seen," said Ron out loud. He held the rod steady and lowered a nymph into the dark water. The fish took it, just like that. He just bit down on the hook and waited. Ron tugged.

It was unnatural. Holding the fly gently between his ugly lips, the fish lifted his head out of the pool and looked up at Ron with an old, dim eye.

Then, effortlessly, he spit the hook out of his mouth. Ron's heart thunked.

The cutthroat looked like it was wearing armor, it was so old and tough. Not scaly exactly, but covered with a crust that looked as hard as toenails. Ron ran his finger along the three parallel scars on its back.

"Osprey," the fish said. "When I was just a small fry."

Ron jerked his hand away.

"Picked me up and dropped me near here. The pond I was living in almost dried up. My lucky day."

"Fish don't talk," said Ron. He took off his glasses and wiped them with his shirt, not sure if it was his eyes or his ears that were deceiving him.

"I'm not talking," said the fish. "I'm just thinking."

"Thinking?"

"About the old days. Wild water, and plenty of it. A lady fish who used to live in an eddy around here. Those were the days."

"I know the feeling, said Ron. "But I don't know if she really likes me, this one. She says I'm goofy. It's not enough for me."

"Enough is too much. At least you're communicating," the fish said, its voice liquid and dreamingly gurgly.

"Yeah, but *goofy?* It's not exactly a compliment," Ron said. "I don't know how to respond."

"Tell her this," the fish said.

"This is crazy. Fish don't talk."

"I'm not talking. I'm thinking. Bend down. Listen."

So Ron did.

THE FRUGAL FRAMER

I have never wronged any person nor taken that which was not mine.

Norman Sanger

Hugh and Brenda are talking about leaving town again. The Frugal Framer, Switchback's picture framing shop, is located in their house, one block over from Main. Is the house in the shop, or is the shop in the house? After all this time you can't tell where one ends and the other begins, what with the way one invades the other. A sandwich on a plate sits on the front counter next to the samples of cardboard mat. A splendid oil painting of the Ruby River Valley hangs over their bed, waiting to be picked up some day by a cowboy who went to Argentina a couple of years ago. They haven't heard from him, but just in case he shows up again, his picture is ready. They've had it so long that Brenda has bought a quilt in colors to match. It brings the room together.

"We thought about calling our shop the Frantic Framer," explained Hugh to a customer one day. "But then people might think we're speedy. We like to take our time."

"We don't like to be rushed," Brenda agreed. *"The longer you wait, the better we look.* That's our motto." Hugh nodded in agreement.

It's right after the first big snowfall every year that they talk of leaving. December does that to people in cold climates. It is not an optimistic season. In a town like Switchback, winter does not offer the entertainment that you might find in a bigger city, diversions that take your mind off the coming gloom. There are no festivals or celebrations, just one night of fifty-cent drafts and free cake down at the Fry Pan on Vern's birthday. The Ben Franklin store stocks up on sequins and hot glue guns for people who like to make their own holiday presents, but for the most part, winter is when you talk about how you wished you lived in Hawaii. Arizona. Florida. Hugh and Brenda talk about it more than most folks. They are in their sixties now and shoveling snow one hundred and four (he has counted) days a year does not seem like something to brag about. He is no longer proud of it. He feels stupid that he ever boasted about it in the first place.

December brings Switchback people together. You can't garden when you get home from work; the ground is frozen and it's pitch dark. So you cultivate conversations instead, working the aisles at the Village Market like you would a cocktail party if you lived in a more civilized place. You feel a need to mingle.

Good-byes become difficult. You think about death more. Who knows when you'll see these people again? Even if they live only a few blocks away, you never know, do you? What if this very friend keels over in a snowdrift outside of town next week, or is killed by the cold some frigid night, changing a flat tire on the pass? Just because it hasn't happened in years doesn't mean it couldn't, again.

There's still that old *Tailings* article on the wall of the Valley Forge, that tells how in 1899, Ezekiel Goddard went out to check his cows and froze to his shovel handle before his wife missed him. That's winter for you.

Ron Martinez, while looking for his space heater, came across a small, unsigned watercolor painting of Echo Mountain that he'd found stuck into a book at the library sale last summer. The snowfields above timberline were pink. He took it to The Frugal Framer to consult with Hugh and Brenda.

"Haven't seen you much since last year," said Hugh. "How'd your mom like that picture you gave her?"

"Liked it fine," Ron said. "She loves anything with frogs. This year I made her a step stool. This here is for someone else." He handed Hugh the painting.

"Nice," Hugh said admiringly. "It's a good thing you're bringing it in now. This is our final winter here." He sounded like he meant it.

"I think you said that last year," Ron commented.

"But this time it's true. Last year we weren't really ready. We decided we needed the extra time to bring the place up to snuff so it'll show better. Say, let me ask your opinion," Hugh continued. "What do you think we should do to spruce this place up so it looks good? You know...more salable?"

Ron looked around the shop. Racks of molding, mat samples, a huge paper cutter. You had to squeeze yourself against the wall to walk around the chopper in the back room. It looked like what it was, a busy workplace with living quarters in the back.

"You would have to empty it out and re-paint. People like an empty place so they can imagine their own stuff in here. They'd probably want to make a second bedroom out of the back room," Ron offered. "My mom used to be in real estate. That's what she told her sellers."

"That's the assembly room. What's the matter with them?" bristled Hugh. "Don't they have any imagination?" Hugh and Brenda, as artists, were capable of seeing beyond the obvious. "We were kind of hoping that someone who wants a frame shop would come by and want it just the way it is."

"That might limit your options," Ron said gently. "Where you moving to?"

"We're not completely sure. Wyoming, probably," said Hugh.

"Wyoming's too cold," Brenda piped up from the kitchen. "Colorado Springs."

"We want to get away from all these people," said Hugh, waving abstractly out at Third Avenue, where at that moment, a lone man and a dog were staring up the street, as if waiting for a lift.

"We want to be near an airport," Brenda's voice again. Brenda had relatives, including an aging mother, in the East. "I'm not moving way the hell out in the middle of nowhere again."

"We're still in the discussion stage," Hugh explained. "But this is the last winter, definitely."

"Well, lots of people miss you," Ron said. "You're real locals. Didn't someone call you guys the spiritual guideposts of Switchback once?"

Hugh snorted. "Mackerel snappers." But it was too late to change any of that now, since Monsignor Delaney's visit.

Hugh and Brenda are agnostics, perhaps even atheists. The name of the Lord simply does not come up for them, in vain or otherwise. They are non-religious. They do not attend church except for the occasional wedding or funeral. They do not tithe. They go to the church carnival on St. Teresa's lawn in August, along with everyone else in town, and Brenda donates hand-painted Christmas cards each December for their bazaar. You don't have to be Catholic to do that.

In the old days there was a rectory next to St. Teresa's, but it burned down years ago, right after the mine closed. At the same time, a lot of people left town, including most of the Catholics. The Archdiocese of Denver, in its wisdom, decided that it wasn't worth the price of wood to build a house for a full-time priest again. Let young Father Tony drive up on Sundays to say mass. He had a nice house by St. Mary's in Aspen on Galena Street, a season ski pass, a new pair of skis and an SUV with a cross painted on the door.

Hugh's and Brenda's place sits right next to St. Teresa's, in the shadow of the steeple. No one feels ill-at-ease with unbelievers living so close. Parishioners park in front of their building during Sunday mass, and once Father Tony called Hugh on the phone to get him to crawl in the back window to look for his American Express card, which he thought he might have dropped during the recessional.

Living next to the Catholic Church, Hugh and Brenda have learned, carries with it certain implied responsibilities.

First there was the red-faced professor from a Catholic College in the Midwest. Who knows what he was doing in Switchback anyway? He just got into his Ford and drove, I-70 through Denver to Colorado 82, turned left at Glenwood Springs and kept taking side roads, clutching the wheel with meaty, pink hands, wishing he had the courage to run himself off the road. Sixty-two years old, nothing in the world to show for himself but this rusty old car, and his students laughed at him. And why not? He was old and dull; he had no wife, children or bank account. How can you come so far and be so worthless? There was no meaning to it all.

People who are not so devout might talk over their problems of depression with a friend. Or maybe, if they are of the modern generation, they might do like the talk show psychologists recommend and seek therapy. But this man, a Catholic of the old school, only knew that he needed to see a priest.

He pulled to a stop in front of St. Teresa's, where the pavement ends. The lights in what looked like a rectory next door were on. Feeling somewhat calmer now that spiritual help was in sight, he knocked, and Hugh, The Frugal Framer, let him in.

Two hours later, a dinner of meatloaf and potatoes au gratin under his belt (Brenda's specialty) and a good conversation about the meaning of life, the professor checked into the motel next to Guns 'n' Jewels Pawn Shop and slept ten hours straight. Like a baby. When he awoke, he wasn't exactly sure where he was, but the sign outside pointed to Glenwood Springs and he knew from there he could get to Denver and, eventually, home. Today when he tells the story, he is not even certain why the kind priest's living room was filled with picture framing tools, or why he and his housekeeper, whose meatloaf was excellent, seemed so affectionate towards each other. It was not his place to ask. They didn't call it the Wild West for nothing, he figured.

Another time, it was the nuns. It was a shock when they were told that their small Denver convent had been sold to a real estate developer, and the archbishop suggested that before reporting to their new post in Kremmling, they take a week off, relax. It was a summer afternoon when their van came to a stop in front of The Frugal Framer and Sister Mary Edward asked for directions to the rectory. Once, she explained, when she first entered the novitiate, she remembered hearing that a high mountain town called Switchback was looking for some sisters to run a school there for the children of the parish.

"Oh, dear," Brenda said. "I'm afraid that was a very long time ago."

"I seem to remember that The Sound of Music came out just a few years prior," Sister Mary Edward said. "I saw the priest's letter..."

"That would have been Father Lawrence," said Brenda.

"... and pictured myself dancing in circles in some high mountain meadow in a dirndl. I was living in Cleveland at the time."

Brenda explained that the only priest they had now was Father Tony, and he wouldn't be showing up for six days, to say mass on Sunday.

Sister Mary Edward and the others took a look around them. It was that one week in the summer when the bluebells grow so thick in the ditches that you can't even see the water, the week when you can stand in one spot and count fifteen, twenty different varieties of wildflowers without even turning your head. Hugh crawled in the back window of the church and unlatched the side door for them, and by nightfall, the sisters were settled in, sleeping one to each narrow pew. Early the next morning, hitching their habits above their ankles, they explored a high meadow pink with watermelon snow, where the air was so thin it made their hearts beat wildly, almost like they were in love.

Mothers brought their children to St. Teresa's every afternoon that week and the sisters told them stories and led them in art projects using stuff they'd picked up along the road. Giggling with their ineptitude, they tried to weave baskets out of willow branches and make little boats from pieces of bark. They taught the children the words to *Edelweiss*.

Switchback is often a sweet place, but that week was the sweetest of all. In the evenings after the setting of the sun, folks would find an excuse to sit on their porches, listening for the clear, high voices of five sisters singing in the darkness. The morning customers at the Fry Pan watched their language that week, because Sister Martha came in every day for a thermos of coffee, and no one wanted to see her black-and-white-clad figure out of the corner of his eye just as he was wrapping up a dirty joke.

On their last day, Brenda walked with the sisters up along the river called the Tumbling Falls, and they picked chokecherries from branches that hung heavy over the water. Then they returned to the Frugal Framer and made jam, staining their fingers with indelible red juice.

Over the years, Hugh's and Brenda's has been a source of refuge for many. When Trina thought she was pregnant, before she and Bob were married, they found her sitting on their stoop, wondering. When old Oscar's brother got cancer and thought a bit of prayer might be in order, he found the church door locked, but the Frugal Framer had the Open sign up, and Brenda was just pulling some biscuits out of the oven. Brenda's biscuits were as good as any prayer.

The archbishop came up from Denver to celebrate the Confirmation mass with the youngsters last year, and after the ceremony, in which he gave each child a gentle slap on the cheek, signifying that he or she was now a soldier of Christ, he knocked on the door of The Frugal Framer, having heard so much about its owners. An hour and a half later, when Edna Spivak came over to remind him of the celebration dinner at the Continos, she found him in his shirtsleeves, leaning back in an old kitchen chair, asking Hugh for his thoughts on papal infallibility, his ecclesiastical robes bunched up in a heap on the floor.

Hugh and Brenda's friend, Linda, who lives in a town called Palisade, four thousand feet lower in elevation with two extra months of growing season a year, sends them real estate catalogs to read. Palisade, Linda writes, is how Switchback used to be.

"But Switchback is still like Switchback used to be," says Brenda in its defense. "It's just too damned cold. And too far from my family. And that snooty golf course crowd is a pain in the butt."

"I thought you said you wanted to move," Linda argues. "I'm just trying to help you make up your minds."

"Where could we go that's as good as here?"

"Wyoming," bellows a male voice, barely audible over the scream of an electric saw cutting through oak. "As soon as the snow melts.

POTICA

"Talk about bad luck," Ron said over the phone. "My interview with the bat guano guy got cancelled. It was going to be a full ten-minute piece, the whole last part of my show."

"Play music instead," Katie suggested. She held the phone to one ear as she cracked walnut shells over a plate.

"You mean, like, Christmas music? I don't have time to pick anything out. Besides, this is a talk show. People listen to me because I talk. I tell stories."

"That's what I like about you," Katie said.

"I thought you said I was goofy."

"You are. But not in a bad way."

"You have to take the goofy with the sufi," Ron said.

Katie blinked hard. "Where'd you hear that?" she asked.

"An ancient master said it."

"Who? Rumi? Rabindernath Tagore?"

"No, a local."

"I'd like to give that some thought," said Katie solemnly.

"Later. Right now I need your help. Remember that story you read to me? The one you wrote about your grandmother?"

"Potica. I'm making it today. I'm just about to grind the walnuts."

"That's the one. You said it was a Christmas story. The timing is perfect. Would you come down and read it? I need you in fifteen minutes."

"Fifteen minutes! That's not enough time!"

"Enough is too much," Ron countered. "C'mon. I'm just down the block at the studio. You can be here in no time. Listen, all you have to do is read it into the microphone. I'll do the rest."

"But what if someone *hears* it?" Katie asked. "What if someone is listening?"

"This is KSWT," Ron said. "Only Switchback is listening, and not that many of them. They'll mostly be down at the Valley Forge for the gingerbread cook-off.

"Oh, yeah, well, I don't know. This is scary..."

"Just be here! Please? Please please please?" Ron had a way with words. *"Please?"*

"Would you take me to dinner at a fancy restaurant?" said Katie.

"Huh? Sure. If that's what you want. But wouldn't you rather go camping?"

"Yes. Just kidding. I'll be right down."

And that is how Katie came to read her first story on the radio.

THE POTICA STORY
As read on KSWT

I guess it's my imagination. But I thought I just heard my grandmother's voice ask: "Did you make your potica yet?"

Yes, Gram. I did. It came out of the oven an hour ago. All the hours I was grinding those walnuts, all the time I waited for the dough to rise and then rolled it out, you were leaning over my shoulder, making sure I didn't forget anything. If there's one day a year you come back to haunt me, it's the day I make potica.

Potica is a nut-filled bread that's baked in Slovenia, my grandmother's homeland, for holidays. Making potica is time consuming and physically demanding. The dough must be kneaded for hours, just long enough for your elbows to start squeaking The walnuts must be painstakingly ground many times to make a smooth paste. (Grandma called this paste "moosh.") There are no shortcuts to making potica. It takes at least a day out of your life.

But Christmas isn't Christmas in my family unless there's potica. We would sooner go without presents than without a slice of that sweet, rich dessert.

That's why, when I was seventeen, I thought I'd better learn to make potica myself. So I went to see Grandma.

"Gram, may I have the recipe for potica?" I asked.

"There is no recipe. You chust make it," said my grandmother.

"What do you mean," You just make it?" I demanded. I had a rudimentary knowledge of baking, having once made a loaf of bread on a bet. Baking, I knew, takes recipes.

"It's easy," said my grandmother. "It's chust like bread."

So I went home and got out that bread recipe. Flour, water, yeast, shortening, salt, sugar. I let the dough rise, rolled it out, put ground walnuts on it (remembering smugly how they had to be ground fine enough to be moosh.) I rolled it up and baked it.

"It's like a brick," my grandmother said when she bit into it. How much milk did you put in?"

"Milk? You didn't say anything about milk! I made it with water. 'Just like bread,' you said."

"Well, next Christmas when you make your potica, put in milk," Gram said simply. "And you have to knead it good and hard. All morning, almost."

Another Christmas rolled around. Now that I knew the secret, I was ready to tackle potica a second time. I asked my mom to have the milkman deliver an extra half-gallon of milk.

I kneaded till the muscles knotted on my arms and sweat ran down my face. I ground up those walnuts till they were a gooshy moosh. And when it came out of the oven, it wasn't a brick. But it didn't taste like potica, either.

"Taste this," I demanded when Grandma came over for Christmas Eve. "This isn't potica."

Gram had one nibble and agreed. "You forgot to put the cinnamon," she stated flatly.

"No one said anything about cinnamon. You just said there were walnuts in the filling!"

"Well" she said. "There's cinnamon too. And a little honey."

That was simple enough. Cinnamon and honey. I could remember that. So the following year, two weeks before Christmas, I telephoned my grandmother long-distance from my new home, Colorado. "Let's make this quick," I said. "It's my nickel. Now, I have milk. I have cinnamon. I have honey, I have walnuts..."

"Grind them up fine, to make a moosh," she offered.

"I made a moosh!" I almost shouted. "I have sugar, yeast, salt, butter. Is there anything else?"

There was a silence at the other end of the line. "Eggs," she said, pronouncing it "X". She whispered, reluctant to divulge such valuable information after only four years of interrogation.

"X," I repeated, stunned. "You never told me X. You should have told me eggs the first year. How come you never said eggs before?"

"You didn't ask," Gram said.

Eight or nine years went by. Every December, I'd telephone my grandmother and run down the list of ingredients. Every year, she'd reveal one more secret spice or technique.

But it finally happened. My years of persistence paid off. I finally made a potica that tasted just like Grandma's. Finally, almost a decade from my first try, I had made a potica that would have made Frankie Yankovich, The Polka King, break out into *She's Too Fat For Me*. My filling was rich, my dough had just the right amount of honey and milk, the color was perfect and the texture divine.

I wrapped one up in tinfoil and sent it to Grandma parcel post.

"Did you taste it?" I asked her when I called a few days later. "Wasn't it great? I put in cinnamon. I put in eggs. I made a moosh. I brushed the top with butter and egg yolk. What do you think?"

"Pretty good," admitted Grandma. "It's almost right."

"What do you mean, ALMOST?" I demanded. "It's perfect! How can you tell me it's *almost* right?"

"Because you forgot the lemon rind," she said, rolling the R of rind with a queenly brogue.

"You never said anything about lemon rind!"

"AHA!" said Grandma. Which, in Slovenian, means ho ho ho.

THE DEADLY BLIGHT

"*Western Trends Magazine*? May I speak to Miss Montblanc, please? Natasha? Miss Montblanc? This is Katie. You know, the Potato Day story? Switchback?"

"Katie! Still working in that fabulous little boutique? I got the most marvelous cashmere coat there."

"Great. Say, Eudora, about the story...something's come up," Katie said, her voice deep with regret.

"Come up?"

"They told me not to say anything about it. The publicity and all. But, just between you and me, something horrible has happened."

"No!" Katie could hear Eudora reaching for her pen.

"It's the blight. The deadly potato blight."

"Deadly?"

"*Deadly.* Three people."

"Why hadn't I heard about it?"

"They're trying to keep it quiet. Besides, they didn't actually die...at least not *yet.* It is a long, lingering illness, quite degenerative, I'm afraid. *Ghastly,*" she added, dramatically.

"Ghastly," Eudora echoed.

"They traced it back to the potatoes they ate at the Potato Day barbecue in the park. Seems there's a deadly virus up here that contaminated them. They're canceling the whole event, forever. There's lawsuits left and right."

"My God."

"So...in your own interest...I think maybe you might not want to run the story. Liability and all."

"God, you're right. We don't want anyone going up there on our recommendation and contracting the...what do they call it?"

"DPB. Diarrheal Potato Blight. I'm sorry to be the one to break the news to you," Katie said, "but... If you want to verify the story, I have some numbers here, people you can call."

"Okay. Shoot. I'll keep it under my hat, though. We would have looked like damned fools," Eudora said.

"Yeah. Here's the first name. The potato expert. Dr. Ronald Martinez. He's heading the investigative team. They're shut up in a lab wearing gas masks and doing tests. All extremely hush hush, of course."

"Martinez. OK. Hush hush. Anyone else?"

"Sage Wozniak. It's her firm that's handling the class action suit. As you can imagine, people are really furious. Even the gangs..."

"Gangs?"

"Didn't I tell you about the gangs? You'd be amazed. It's like East L.A. up here on a Friday night. You wouldn't believe it."

"They're all over, hon. And listen, about that story...I could arrange a kill fee for you."

"No, really, I just couldn't. I'm sorry it didn't work out. Maybe another time."

"Maybe, but not in that hole. I always thought the name was horrid. Switchback. Sounds like some kind of deadly weapon."

THE CANDLE

Wet leaves lined the still-green grass along the ditch in Wilson Park when Katie stepped down from the bus. The sprinkle of blackbirds at the top branches of the old elms looked like poppy seeds on a bread roll. The late-October sun was just dropping behind the hill. The air smelled of woodsmoke.

Sunlight reached from below the horizon and spread slashes of light that pierced the clouds like the fingers of an open hand. For a few minutes, the park's treetops were lit from below, illuminating the undersides of a few leaves that still clung to branches. A noisy chevron of Canada geese flew across the darkening sky.

It was an evening for kicking through leaves, thought Katie, and there was no one in the park to see her. Folks were inside with their suppers, like she herself would be in a few minutes. She'd put on an old sweater and light the stove, and maybe heat up some water for tea as the place warmed up. She'd check the mailbox out front for a letter.

Katie heard the men's voices before she saw them, at the far end of the park. As she came closer, a few of them nodded at her. Most kept working, raking the bottom of a long pit in the earth that seemed to have been opened up for the occasion. Katie peeked into the hole, its length four times the height of a man, and its width about half that. The rectangular hole was lined with black, ash-charred bricks. At the bottom, four feet down, red coals glowed.

Katie stayed well back of the action to watch. Two men slid some boards out of the back of a pickup and laid them across a pair of ancient sawhorses. Half a dozen ice chests were opened to reveal big chunks of beef that were lifted one by one onto the homemade plank table. Salt, pepper and barbecue sauce appeared. A trio of men set to work preparing the meat for roasting. The first man selected a roast and rubbed salt and paper into it. He passed it the next fellow, who doused the meat with barbecue sauce from a bottle and rolled it up in a long, clean cloth. One at a time, the roasts were passed over to a third man, who wrapped a flexible square of chicken wire around each slab, forming it around the meat, holding the bundle together.

Meanwhile, the men with rakes were smoothing out the bed of ash at the bottom of the pit. Finally, when the job was done to their satisfaction, they stepped back and watched as the roasts—twenty-five or thirty in all—were lowered onto the ash with a hook attached to a long pole that looked home-made expressly for this purpose.

"The meat stays clean because it's all wrapped up," explained one of the men to Katie even before she asked. Someone lowered several roasting pans of foil-wrapped potatoes into the hole, and then two heavy iron doors were placed over the top of the pit, one alongside the other. Only then did two of the men remove their beat-up cowboy hats and wipe the sweat from their faces.

Now everyone grabbed a shovel and began to pile dirt over the top, and then someone passed around a bottle. Katie took a sip, to be polite, mostly.

"Check for leaks," someone said, and the lights of a pickup truck were aimed at the now-closed pit. A think wisp of steam appeared near one end, and someone grabbed a shovel to cover it with more dirt.

"Now what?" Katie asked.

"Now we wait."

"Wait?"

"Tomorrow we shovel off the dirt, open 'er up. We take out the roasts with that long hook and flip them over to the table there. Someone pulls off the chicken wire and saves it for next time. Someone unrolls the cloth and unwraps the meat. Then the roasts are sliced—chopped up, mostly—and that's what we all have for lunch tomorrow. Barbecue on a bun. All you can eat, and spuds, too."

"What if you keep it buried too long?" Katie asked.

"It can't cook too long. As long as the meat doesn't touch the hot coals, it won't burn. The coals burn down to ash and then cool off. It's always just right. There's no rare or medium rare here. There's just *done.* And as tender as a baby's…well, *real* tender."

Katie asked, "How long have you guys been doing this? Those bricks look pretty old."

"Since I can remember."

"You did this when you were little?"

"My dad and granddad did it. They let me throw a couple logs on."

"And tomorrow it gets eaten?" Katie asked.

"Just after the Potato Day parade. Just like always."

"Can anyone come?"

"Sure. Even city girls," said a skinny old guy in coveralls. Katie thought she saw him wink. "Your name's Katie, ain't it?"

Dear Jill,

Tomorrow is Potato Day in Switchback. Back a hundred years ago, half the towns in this part of the state had Potato Days, but Switchback is the only one that still does it anymore. You can smell the barbecue from my house. It's cooking even now. Tomorrow, the cowboys open up the pit and reach down with a hook on a pole, slinging huge slabs of beef off the ashes and onto old wooden tables. They will unwrap the roasts, cut them into chunks, pull the meat apart and serve it up. They'll lift out the huge pans of baking potatoes as well. That's the menu, basically, that and whatever shows up on the potluck table. Me, I'm bringing applesauce. I have enough of it to feed half the town, thanks to that tree of Ida's.

The social scene is different here, if you can call it that. Mostly you go to someone's house with some kind of food to share, and you hear a lot of stories. Folks aren't so afraid of being weird here. It almost helps.

Last week I went to a party down the street with my neighbor, Ron, a nice guy. The son of the hosts is named Dylan and was visiting from college. He is graduating soon with a major in international affairs. Next summer, he's going to Brussels to study economics, and after that he intends to work for the United Nations.

Twenty-one years old and he knows where he's going; he has it all figured out. It made me envious. Why didn't I ever have a plan like that? If you had asked me when I was that age what I expected from life, I would have thought of the hope chest advertisement in *Seventeen* magazine, the one that ran every month on the inside front cover. In it, a young woman in a formal dress and a sparkling wedding ring leans over her beautifully-set dining room table to light the candles. She touches the flame to the last perfect taper as happy guests, men in suits and women in evening gowns, begin walking through the door, laughing, as if someone just said something clever. In the foreground of the scene there is a hope chest. Remember those things? Mom still has one up in the attic. It smells like cedar, like a hamster cage.

That's how I thought life would be. I would marry, have a nice house and great clothes and I would light the candles as the guests walked in the door. I didn't consider that the food must be purchased and prepared. I didn't know who was paying the rent. Those things would be taken care of if only I was dressed up and ready to light those candles.

But around the time I was seventeen myself, something began to gnaw at me. I wanted to be an artist like Grandma, or maybe a writer. I wanted adventure. I didn't want perfect-looking friends like the people in the ad. They looked like they would talk about real estate values and fancy vacations. One day, looking at the current issue's hope chest advertisement, I imagined the entire dinner party unfolding. The men would brag about their cars. The women would compliment my dinnerware or talk about who did their hair. I hated their superficiality. It was all I could do to endure their inane, predictable witticisms, even in my own daydream, and I resolved never to invite them back. The whole picture scared me.

But Dylan, the kid down the street, doesn't seem scared. He has the blueprint of his whole life drawn up already. It is as ordered as an interstate map, with smooth lines leading from point A to point B. Why wasn't I like that? No, if my life plan were a map, it would look like a dog-eared pirate's chart complete with shipwrecks, witch doctors and convoluted dotted-line routes, some leading to dead ends. Some plan, huh? Now that I am grown, I am embarrassed at my naiveté.

Remember the story of the grasshopper and the ant? It was a television cartoon when I was little, before you were born. Dad used to say I was like the grasshopper.

While the ants plodded away, storing food for the winter, marching in industrious rows from dawn until dark, the grasshopper played his fiddle and danced, never worrying about tomorrow.

Yes, I admitted to Dad, I am a grasshopper. Guilty as charged. But even if all they do is fiddle, every spring they're back again. Plan or no plan, they survive.

Do you think he really wanted me to be an ant? A nurse or a school teacher? Would it have made him more proud? Maybe. I think so.

"Jack of all trades, master of none." The first time I heard that expression, I didn't know what it meant. What was a jack of all trades? Mom had to explain it to me. That's for me! I thought. Someone who knew a little bit about everything! Unlike the stylish guests in my dinner party daydream, I wanted quantity instead of quality. A classier person wants it the other way around, doesn't she? But not me. I want messy variety, a gypsy caravan of stuff and experience. I wanted foreign lands, poets, Bohemian friends, adventure.

So here I am, wondering if I should have been more-- well, more *focused.* My employment history includes: secretary, school teacher, dishwasher, pet sitter, columnist, maid, business owner, bookkeeper, instructor of shorthand and macramé, waitress, mistress, translator, bartender, event chairman, fund raiser, designer, shop girl, volunteer, DJ, inventor, naturalist, quilter, caterer, storyteller, librarian, guitar teacher, singer, actress, machine embroiderer, nurses aide, folk singer. Every time I tried something new, I wondered if Dad was looking down on me, shaking his head and saying sadly: *Grasshopper.*

My role models were all artists and eccentrics. Grandma, Willa Cather, Zorba, Georgia O'Keefe, Marco Polo, T.E. Lawrence. Each in his or her own way left a body of work. Some left volumes of literature, others, like Grandma, rooms full of art. You look at their work and you know what they were all about. My own body of work, if you dare to call it that, is as varied as the discards in Theodora's bargain room. It includes a few poems, a shrine made out of a television set, some stories written in notebooks, a well-mulched garden, some trees I helped plant in Wilson Park, and many enchiladas, fruit pies and poticas brought to pot lucks. There is KSWT, where I am just a volunteer, but every time I turn on the radio, I feel like I help keep that station on the air. There are paintings I did of Evelyn Store Road and villages in England. A book of lyrics, the music still in my head. Some day maybe I'll organize it all, but in the meantime I want to go next door and see Ida. She promised me some cuttings from her African violets after I roll up her hoses and drag them into the garage for her. First things first.

You get the drift. I lack the singular, laser-like focus of a successful person. Without a career, I have failed to fulfill my potential.

But last night I had a dream. You were in it, too. We were all there---you and I and mom and dad, both the grandmas, Eric and Ron. It was my birthday, and in honor of the event, Dad was going to show home movies of my life. He got out his old sixteen-millimeter Bell and Howell projector but he couldn't find the screen. He tried to project onto the wall, but they still had that atrocious foil wallpaper we had in the sixties, remember? So he decided he would turn the lens upward and project the movies on the ceiling.

But--there was no ceiling. It was missing entirely, and when you looked up to where it should have been, you saw the dark night sky with clouds drifting overhead. Dad flipped the switch and we watched a three-second clip of me at four years old, in the wading pool, projected on a moving cloud. Then the cloud passed and there was nothing but blackness, the projector beaming, imageless, into space. Another cloud passed overhead and the film projected on it my first day of school. That cloud too blew away as quickly as it had come. And on and on. We watched my life in disconnected bits and pieces, projected for a flash in time on a screen of wispy clouds. We looked up and laughed, all of us.

I used to think I was different from other people, never having settled on one thing. But now I see that a lot of folks are like that, at least in this town. We have all traveled convoluted paths that somehow intersect in this tiny spot at this very moment. And, like they have been waiting for a listener all along, people bring me their best stories, which I project, for an instant, on a passing cloud.